"Nick, I can't do thi[s]

"Why not?"

"Because you're not the kind of man—"

"Not the kind of man you should want? God, Sara, you're dying for a man like me."

"Nick—"

"A man who can't wait to drive you absolutely wild in ways you can't even imagine. You want all those things as much as you want your next breath, Sara. And that's exactly what I'm going to give you."

Pulling her forward, he smothered her mouth in a kiss. He held her tightly, his kiss raw and hot and possessive; he made her mind go blank and her insides turn to mush.

So this is what it's supposed to feel like.

Sara thought about the other kisses she'd experienced over the years, those bland, boring, halfhearted attempts that had been cool and hesitant and had left her dying for more. Dying for *this.* And now she wondered what other wondrous things might be out there that she'd been missing all her life.

She had a feeling this man knew every one of them.

Dear Reader,

The moment this story came to mind, I couldn't wait to write it. Nick Chandler is my favorite kind of bad boy, one whose good looks, abundance of charm and killer smile are so disarming that he can talk his way into any woman's heart.

But what happens when the woman Nick wants is Sara Davenport, a psychologist who has written a book that teaches other women how to resist heartbreakers like him? And what happens when the expert on avoiding the bad boy falls for him herself?

The conflict between the good girl and the bad boy is always such fun to write. I hope you enjoy the story!

Visit my Web site at www.janesullivan.com for news of future releases, or write to me at jane@janesullivan.com. I'd love to hear from you!

Best wishes,

Jane Sullivan

Books by Jane Sullivan

HARLEQUIN TEMPTATION
854—ONE HOT TEXAN
898—RISKY BUSINESS
960—TALL, DARK AND TEXAN

HARLEQUIN DUETS
33—STRAY HEARTS
48—THE MATCHMAKER'S MISTAKE

Jane Sullivan

WHEN HE WAS BAD...

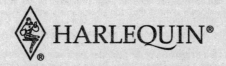

HARLEQUIN®

TORONTO • NEW YORK • LONDON
AMSTERDAM • PARIS • SYDNEY • HAMBURG
STOCKHOLM • ATHENS • TOKYO • MILAN • MADRID
PRAGUE • WARSAW • BUDAPEST • AUCKLAND

To my editor, Jennifer Green.
Thank you for your enthusiasm about my books,
your editorial advice that always improves them, and your sense of humor that makes my life as a writer a whole lot more fun. I love writing for Harlequin, and you're the reason why.

ISBN 0-373-69202-1

WHEN HE WAS BAD...

Copyright © 2004 by Jane Graves.

www.eHarlequin.com

Printed in U.S.A.

1

He's a daredevil on a motorcycle, a rebel with his own cause, a careless heartbreaker or an intriguing man of mystery.

He's a handsome devil with a buff bod, or a tattooed badass spoiling for a fight. He's a seductive charmer who will bring out the best in you.

And the worst.

He's a self-absorbed loner, aloof and jealous and tantalizingly possessive, attracting you with enough charisma for ten men; at the same time, he holds you at arm's length.

Caught up in the thrill of the chase, you try to grasp his heart and soul, only to feel him slipping away like sand through your fingers.

And while you know you should resist, with just a crook of his finger and a devastating smile, off you go with him, your mind filled with delusions of taming this enigmatic man. And when he has you melting under his hypnotic gaze, falling so fast your head is spinning, that's when he leaves you like a shadow in the night, never to be seen again…

SARA DAVENPORT knew every one of those men inside and out. She could quote their characteristics, chapter and verse—every nuance of behavior, every game they played, every brand of falsehood that passed their lips. After all, she'd written the book on bad boys.

Literally.

She took a sip of coffee, then sat back on the sofa in her office and spread her planner out in her lap. Next to her, Karen paged through her own planner, lining out their schedule for the coming week.

"I've set up book signings for Wednesday and Thursday evening," Karen told her. "They're here in Boulder, so there's no travel involved." She flipped to another page. "I arranged a phone interview for you with a regional magazine in Charleston. The reporter will e-mail you tomorrow to set up a time. And I booked you for a Friday evening Internet chat with a reader's group in Spokane."

Sara made a few notes. "Wow. You're keeping me busy."

Karen smiled. "Busy is good. It won't be long before your name is a household word."

Sara didn't doubt that. Her friend's PR wizardry was a big reason the book had been successful so far. Karen knew just which newspapers and magazines to target with advance reading copies to garner the most articles and reviews. She'd brought Sara untold numbers of new readers by suggesting she pair a minilecture with book signings. She'd gotten her a cameo in *Cosmopolitan*. All that publicity had put Sara on the fast track to success, but still it was hard for her to believe that she'd barely turned thirty and already her dream was coming true.

Not that she'd intended for things to work out the way they had. She'd initially envisioned the book as an expansion of her dissertation, a serious examination of the psychological, social and emotional reasons women make poor choices in men. But one year, three edits and a show-stopping cover later, it had become a shorter, slicker book with a pop psychology tone and a title that made her cringe: *Chasing the Bad Boy*.

Sara was still hiding her face over that, but she couldn't argue with success. The book was heading for its third printing, her editor wanted another book and Sara's message was getting out in a way that never would have happened through her private psychology practice or her seminars alone.

"Oh, yeah," Karen said. "One more thing. I called the program director at KZAP this morning."

Sara came to attention. "What for?"

"To book you on a radio show."

Sara felt a surge of apprehension. "Radio? No. I don't want to do radio."

"But you can reach a lot of people on a radio show. And it has an advantage that advertising doesn't."

"What's that?"

"It's free."

"No. Radio is unpredictable. It's too easy to say the wrong thing and get embarrassed."

"Come on, Sara. You're in front of audiences all the time."

"Right. Doing seminars. It's friendly territory. I have notes, and I'm in control. I don't like open-ended situations. They're recipes for disaster."

"You know your subject, and you're a great speaker. What is there to worry about?"

"I just don't want—" Sara stopped short. "Wait a minute. KZAP? Isn't that the station with Dr. Frieda?"

"Yeah."

Okay. Now, maybe that wouldn't be so bad. Discussing her book with a medical doctor, maybe getting into the physiological aspects of attraction, taking questions from her listeners…how tough could that be?

"But I booked you on Nick Chandler's show," Karen said.

For the count of three, Sara's voice deserted her, and when it finally returned, still she could barely get words out without choking.

"*What* did you say?"

"Now, I knew you were going to freak out. But—"

"There is no 'but' here. I'm not getting within ten miles of that man."

"But it'll be great publicity."

"Promoting my book on his show? Are you kidding me?"

"Okay. I know it sounds a little weird, but—"

"A little weird? Do you know he once interviewed a man who claimed he'd had sex with a thousand women and has the notches in his bedpost to prove it?"

"Well, yeah, but—"

"And a woman who tends bar in a topless club? Topless?"

"Yeah, I heard that one. But—"

"And a man who has a Web site dedicated to teaching other men how to *score* with *chicks?*"

Karen held up her palm. "I know. I know. It's a lot of tes-tosterone all in one place, but—"

"I've read the gossip columns. I know Nick Chandler's reputation in this town."

Karen shrugged. "So he gets around a little."

"A little? The guy with the thousand notches in his bed-post is an *amateur* compared to him!"

"And that's exactly the reason I booked you on his show."

Sara took a deep breath and tried to calm down, but it was a hard-won battle. Publicity was a good thing, but Nick Chandler wasn't. The man was so Neanderthal that his knuckles had to drag the ground. Sara shuddered. He probably had back hair and bad posture and drew pictures of bison on his apartment walls.

"Sorry, Karen. I'm not doing a show like that. Call the producer back and tell him to forget it."

"Even if Nick Chandler has a hundred thousand listeners?"

Sara's lower jaw fell halfway to her lap. "Are you telling me that a hundred thousand people tune in to hear *that* kind of programming?"

"Yep."

"But none of them are going to want to hear about my book. His audience is all men."

"Hell it is. Thirty-two percent women, demographic eighteen to thirty-five. That's thirty-two thousand women who are going to be tuning in Thursday afternoon whether you're there or not."

"Why? So they can be objectified?"

"Sweetie," Karen said, "they tune in for Nick Chandler."

"Come on, Karen! What could a woman possibly find attractive about a man like him?"

"I believe you answered that question in your book."

"Okay, yes, but—"

"I'm guessing you've never seen him."

"No. I haven't had the pleasure."

Karen reached down to Sara's laptop sitting on the coffee table in front of the sofa. She tapped a few keys. A few moments later she turned the computer toward Sara, who looked at the screen and froze.

Holy mother of God.

Right there on the index page of the KZAP Web site sat Nick Chandler, lounging in a chair in the studio, the microphone tugged over to his lips, wearing a warm, open smile that was engaging beyond belief. His rich coffee-brown hair just brushed his collar in the back, and his eyes were such a brilliant shade of blue that gemstones all over the world had to be crying with jealousy. But Sara wasn't fooled. Even as his roguish charm oozed right off the screen, she sensed a hint of overbearing overconfidence that gave away the truth: where women were concerned, he played hard and expected to win.

But although she could tell he was every bit the smooth-talking, women-stalking, commitment-mocking man his reputation said he was, she didn't delude herself. A single glance at him could be hazardous to a woman's heart.

She looked away. "He's…decent-looking."

Karen slumped against the back of the sofa. "Are you kidding me? I'd trade every sex toy in my nightstand drawer for fifteen minutes with a man like him."

"Oh, yeah? And what would you have in the sixteenth minute?"

"One hell of an afterglow."

Sara rolled her eyes.

"I didn't say I wanted to head down the aisle with him," Karen went on. "I said I wanted fifteen minutes of wild, outrageous, multiorgasmic sex."

"Fine. But you know the difference between a one-nighter and a lifetimer. Most women don't. They think they're going to change the way a man like him thinks about women. About love. About life. And that's not going to happen."

"So tell them that."

"And have Nick Chandler smack down every word I say?"

"With luck, that's exactly what he'll do."

"What?"

"Controversy sells," Karen said. "If you go head-to-head with him, we might be able to squeeze all kinds of press out of it. Good girl meets bad boy head-on. Get it?"

"I told you I'm not interested."

Karen gave her a sly smile. "What's the matter? Afraid you can't stay on top of a man like him?"

Sara frowned. "Spare me the innuendo, will you?"

"You wrote that book because of men like him, and now you're afraid to face him?"

"I'm not afraid to face him."

"Good. You shouldn't be. You have at least thirty points of IQ on him."

"How do you know that?"

"Because you have at least thirty points of IQ on everyone."

"Thanks for the vote of confidence, but I'm still not doing that show."

Karen sat back with a heavy sigh. "Sure. Okay. If that's the way you want it."

"That's the way I want it."

Karen tapped her fingers against her planner, then gave Sara an offhand shrug. "I mean, I guess it *is* a lot safer just to keep on preaching to the choir."

"What do you mean by that?"

"I mean that you can keep on talking to those women who pay big bucks at your seminars to hear you tell them what they already know. Or what they're finally ready to hear. Or…" Karen gave her a no-nonsense stare. "You can rescue the wayward souls from the devil himself."

Sara considered that for a moment. Karen was right. It was one thing to help women who knew they needed it. But what about opening the eyes of women who didn't?

"You're sure he has that many women who tune in to his show?" Sara asked.

"Yep. Thirty thousand plus."

"He's exactly the kind of man those women need to stay away from."

"Right. But if they've got the hots for him, it means they need you. Every last lust-filled one of them. Can you think of a better place to talk to your target audience?"

Sara sighed. Going on that show would be a mistake. It had to be, didn't it?

Then again, she had to admit that so far Karen hadn't steered her wrong. Her creativity in promotion knew no bounds.

Neither did her powers of persuasion.

"I'll come along, of course," Karen said. "To give you moral support."

Sara wavered. She really did want to get her book into the hands of as many women as possible. Maybe this was a way to accomplish that.

"Okay," Sara said with a sigh of resignation. "I'll do it."

"Thank God," Karen said with relief. "You fell for it."

"Fell for what?"

"You bought all that 'it'll sell books' stuff. All I really wanted was an excuse to meet Nick Chandler in person."

Sara smiled. "Why? So you can work toward that fifteen minutes?"

"Don't worry. I'll let you have first crack at him. If you decide you don't want him, just toss him my way."

"Come on, Karen. Both of us are smarter than that."

Karen sighed. "Yeah, I know. But that doesn't stop me from wishing sometimes that I was a *dumb* blonde." She glanced at her watch. "I've got to go. There's a bar stool at Kelly's with my name on it." She zipped her planner, then stood up. "Your appointments are over for the day. Why don't you come along?"

"Can't. I need to head home and do a little brainstorming."

"Brainstorming?"

Sara sighed. "I'm having a hard time coming up with a concept for my next book."

"Same subject, different take?"

"Yeah. That's what my editor wants, but I just don't know where to go with it."

"A couple of martinis might break that logjam."

"I'll pass."

"Come on, Sara. When's the last time you and I hit a happy hour together?"

"I've been busy. You've *kept* me busy."

"Hey, I'm all for working hard. But you need your playtime, too. I think you're the one who needs to get laid."

"You know I don't do casual sex."

"Then make it a formal occasion. Evening gown, tiara, the whole thing. Personally, I wouldn't want to get that dressed up just to have a man rip it all off, but if it works for you, go for it."

Sara suppressed a smile. "How did we ever get to be friends, anyway?"

"You know how we got to be friends. We suffered through high school hell together. And speaking of high school hell, how's your mother these days?"

"We met for lunch a few days ago. It's been pretty good between us since she moved back here."

"So she really did leave that creep in St. Louis for good?"

"Looks like it. This is going to be a good holiday, Karen. She's coming over for dinner next week on Christmas Eve, and then we're spending Christmas Day together."

"Good," Karen said, with a smile that looked a little phony. "That's good."

Sara recognized the dubious look on her friend's face.

In the past, it would have been justified. But not anymore. "It's okay, Karen. It's been three months. I think my mother has finally seen the light."

"That's what you thought with the other guys, too."

"I know. But this time she sees the pattern of her behavior and wants to do something about it."

"Hey, you're the shrink. If you say her brain's finally unscrambled where men are concerned, I believe you." She checked her watch. "Oops. Happy hour is starting without me." She rose from the sofa and headed for the door.

"Thanks for all your help, Karen."

"Just stick with me, *dahling*. I'll make you a star."

With a couple of theatrical air kisses tossed Sara's way, Karen swept out of her office and closed the door behind her. Sara glanced back at her computer screen.

Good Lord, what had she just agreed to?

Nick Chandler seemed to be staring right at her, teasing her, taunting her, daring her to walk right into his lair, where he lay in wait to chew her into a thousand tiny pieces.

He was undoubtedly good at ad-libbing. She wasn't. He knew how to commandeer conversations and steer them in the direction he wanted them to go. She didn't. He had those eyes that could knock her train of thought right off its track, while she had not a single body part that could hope to distract a man like him.

What she did have, though, was a mission, one she had yet to stray from. She hadn't gotten this far in life without facing insurmountable odds, and she wasn't going to stop now. Thirty thousand women would be tuning into his show next Thursday, many of whom were heading down the wrong path. This was her chance to show them the right one.

Nick Chandler wasn't going to get the better of her. By the time that show was over on Thursday, he was going to know he'd met his match.

2

By the time Thursday came, Sara's brain was still holding on to her conviction with the tenacity of a bulldog with a bone. Unfortunately, her stomach wasn't faring so well. For the past hour, it had been doing funny little flip-flops that were making her a little nauseous. On top of that, the snow predicted for that afternoon had come through with a vengeance, snaring her and Karen in traffic. They were now almost late, so Sara didn't have time to stop and compose herself, which meant she was pretty much a nervous wreck.

They walked into the lobby of the radio station and told the receptionist who they were. Sara shook the snow off her shoulders, then took her coat off and held it in front of her in a death grip.

"Stop looking so uptight," Karen said.

Sara squeezed her eyes closed. "I told you I didn't want to do this."

"Just don't let him see you sweat."

"I used extrastrength antiperspirant this morning. Think that'll do the trick?"

"Will you take it easy? It's time to let your hair down a little. Get your message out, but have *fun* with it."

Fun? She felt as if she were heading to her own execution.

A few moments later, a man came out to the lobby. He

was balding, in his midforties, wearing a scruffy pair of khakis and a sweatshirt.

"That must be the producer," Karen whispered. "You'll be on in a minute. Just be sure to stick to English when you talk."

"What do you mean?"

"Whenever you get nervous, you slip into geek speak."

"What are you talking about?"

"Big words nobody cares about. Just talk to people." She patted Sara on the arm. "I'll be waiting for you out here."

Take it easy, keep your cool, stay on message, she told herself. How hard could that really be?

The man introduced himself as Butch Brannigan. He hung Sara's coat on a nearby rack, then led her down a long hall. As he swung open the door that led to the studio, her heart beat wildly. She thought she was ready for her first glimpse of Nick Chandler. Unfortunately, his photo on the Web site had barely given a hint of the man in the flesh.

He wore jeans. A ragged V-neck cotton sweater over a white T-shirt. Boots that looked as if they'd been to a war zone and back. He hadn't seen the business end of a razor that morning, or maybe the morning before, either. Few men could pull off the shabby look without appearing unkempt, but Nick merely looked careless and uninhibited. And those eyes. Dear God. In the war between men and women, they were lethal weapons.

He stood up as she came in. "Hi. You must be Sara."

"Yes," she said, extending her hand. "It's a pleasure to meet you."

"No," he said, his lips easing into a captivating smile. "The pleasure's all mine."

He enveloped her hand in a warm, solid handshake, sending goose bumps crawling all the way up her arm.

Then he pulled out her chair. "Have a seat. We'll be on in just a little bit."

His deep, resonant voice meshed perfectly with his seductive smile and his incredible good looks, creating a package of pure temptation that could turn a defenseless woman with low self-esteem into a mindless love slave in a matter of minutes. Fortunately, Sara wasn't defenseless, her self-esteem was thoroughly intact and Nick Chandler was going to have to fill the position of love slave elsewhere.

Butch left the room and slipped back into the glassed-in booth that looked into the studio. "Thirty seconds, Nick."

She sat down, and Nick handed her a set of headphones. After putting them on, she folded her hands on the desk in front of her. Then realizing how uptight that looked, she stuck them in her lap instead.

"Nervous?" Nick asked.

She whipped around. "No. Not at all."

"Ever do radio before?"

"No. This is my first time."

"Ah. A radio virgin." He smiled reassuringly. "Don't worry. I'll be gentle."

Her heart jolted at the mental image *that* created. "It's okay. I've done a lot of interviews." She forced a look of indifference on her face. "This is just one more, right?"

He nodded, still smiling. "Right."

Pleasant tone of voice. Agreeable expression. Nonconfrontational body language. Everything about him said, *You can trust me.* So why was she still so terrified?

Because she'd heard his show before. She knew his point of view. A copy of her book lay on the desk beside him, and she wondered if he'd read anything more than the inside flap copy.

A few seconds later, Nick hit a button and leaned into

the microphone. "Next in the hot seat is Doctor Sara Davenport, author of a book called *Chasing the Bad Boy.* Hi, Sara. Glad you could join us today. You don't mind if I call you Sara, do you? We're pretty informal around here."

She wished she could keep her doctorate wedged between them, along with the title that came with it, but she didn't want to look stuffy. *Just have fun with it*, Karen had told her.

"Of course you can call me Sara. If I can call you Nick."

"Sweetheart," he said with a dazzling smile, "you can call me anything you want to."

Little prickles of awareness danced across the back of her neck. *Stay on your toes.*

"Why don't you give us your book in a nutshell?" Nick said. "Then we'll chat about it."

She took a deep, silent breath. *Here we go.*

"Well, the premise of my book is that there are certain men who some women have a hard time resisting. They're the guys they meet at the gym with the incredible bodies who want them for *their* bodies and nothing else. The mystery men who are here today and gone tomorrow. The amazingly handsome men who sweep women off their feet, then hit on their sisters the moment they leave the room. These men are all very enticing on the outside, but in reality, most of them are immature, reckless and irresponsible, offering nothing to the women who fall for them."

"Wow," Nick said. "So how many men do you think are out there who fit that description?"

Sara blinked with surprise. As if she had an actual number? "Well, I don't know exactly. But obviously not all men are like that."

"So some of them are pretty good guys."

"Of course."

"So it's really just a select few who are causing a whole bunch of problems."

Her heart skipped. "I didn't say there were a *lot* of problems, just—"

"Sara. You wrote an entire book on the subject. Of course there must be a lot of problems. In this country we don't fell trees just for the heck of it, you know."

Sara just stared at him, her heart thumping. What was she supposed to do now? Defend the logger who'd cut the trees to make the materials that the printer had bought so he could commit her words to paper?

"Okay, so let's narrow it down a little," Nick said. "What's the biggest problem you see with this situation between good girls and bad boys?"

"Women think they're going to change men's thought processes. Make them into something they're not."

"So men are inflexible."

"Some of them are."

"But women aren't."

"Well, *some* women are—"

"But they're inflexible about the right things."

This man was turning her mind to mush. "We're talking about men here. Men who have no intention of ever committing, yet women chase them, anyway."

"Because they like the challenge?"

"Yes. Exactly."

"But you don't?"

"What?"

"Like a man who's a challenge."

Sara's nervousness escalated. "This isn't about me."

"Of course it is. You're a woman, aren't you?"

"Well, yes, but—"

"Are you telling me you've never fallen for one of those bad boys?"

"Of course not."

"Hmm," he said. "Maybe you've just never had the opportunity."

The words fell from his lips like warm honey in a slow drip. In spite of the fact that Sara knew exactly what kind of man he was, still her heart beat with a primal kind of attraction she just couldn't quell.

Get it together, or he's going to tear you apart.

"The basis of the problem lies in women's physiological reactions," she explained. "Some women feel a heightened sense of excitement when they're with a man who they know is bad for them. It's a kind of thrill-seeking behavior, and they're physically drawn to it."

"Physically?" Nick said, as his gaze took a slow trip down Sara's body and back up again. "Hmm. I'm not quite sure I'm following you."

That was a lie. He was following every word she spoke, every breath she took, every blink of an eyelash, and she knew why. He was the charming kind of bad boy who seemed innocuous on the surface, even as he used that charm to disarm his victims so he could control every situation. Intellectually, she knew what he was up to. So why was he making her so nervous?

"It's a physical reaction," she said. "They feel a heightened awareness, and there's an increase in heart rate."

Nick nodded, but he looked a little puzzled.

"And an accelerated neurotransmitter response."

His brows pulled together with confusion.

"And a dilation of blood vessels. That causes the skin to flush. Then the perspiration glands become overstimulated—"

Nick held up his palm. "Hold on there, Sara. I'm afraid you're losing me with all that physiological whatever."

Geek speak. Hadn't Karen warned her about that? "All I'm trying to say is—"

"What you're trying to say," Nick said, leaning toward her and pulling his microphone along with him, "is that bad boys make women *hot*. Is that right?"

He focused those gorgeous eyes on hers with the intensity of a laser beam, and all at once Sara felt her heart race, her face flush, her skin prickle and her palms sweat.

She cleared her throat. "I'm merely saying they have a physical reaction when they're with such men. One that's…uh…hard to ignore."

He gave her a sinful smile that said, *Yes, it is, isn't it?*

"The truth is that good boys will date bad girls," Sara said, "but they know who they can take home to Mom. Some women, though, will go to extremes trying to change a man who's never going to change. For men, bad girls are flings. For women, bad boys are projects."

"But like it or not," Nick said, "women want those bad boys you're talking about. Oh, they say they don't. They say they want men who will mind their manners and take out the trash without being told and be kind to their mothers."

"All very wonderful qualities."

"But that's not *all* they want." He gave her a tempting smile. "They want a man who's exciting. Intriguing. Who keeps them guessing. Who changes from one day to the next and leaves them breathless in an attempt to keep up. A man with an erotic edge who makes them feel alive in a way they never have before. What they want," he said in a voice as smooth as glass, "is a man who's just a little…bit…*dangerous.*"

Sara opened her mouth to speak, but nothing came out.

All she could do was stare at him. It was as if the verbal part of her brain had shut down completely.

Nick glanced at the console. "Wow. Look at that. All the lines are lit up. Better see what the folks have to say." He punched a button. "This is Andy in Alto Linda. Hey, Andy. What's up, man?"

"You haven't done the rundown yet," Andy said. "I'm dying to hear this one."

Sara's nerves tightened. The rundown? What was that?

"Yep. You're right, Andy. Thanks for keeping me on track. I'll do that right away."

Sara looked at him questioningly.

"My listeners want to know what you look like," Nick said.

Sara felt a shot of apprehension. "I don't see the relevancy—"

"Oh, it's relevant to them. Believe me."

He kicked back in his chair, put his foot on the desk and dragged the microphone up to his mouth.

"Okay, guys, let me tell you what I'm looking at here. "Sara Davenport is about five-six, one twenty-five. Long, silky brown hair. Gorgeous green eyes. I think they're green, anyway. They're hard to make out with the reflection off her glasses."

She pursed her lips, trying hard not to react.

"Now, don't worry, Sara," Nick went on. "I'm not knocking off any points for those. Contrary to common belief..." He dropped his voice to a sexy drawl. "Men do make passes at girls who wear glasses."

Sara just sat there, astonished that he was saying these things in front of...good God. A hundred thousand people?

"And I'm thinking she's probably..." Nick paused. "Let's see. Thirty-two years old?"

She couldn't stop her eyes from narrowing.

"Oops," Nick said. "Got the evil eye on that. With all those letters after her name, I assumed she had to be older. Turns out she's not old, just smart. Let's try twenty-eight."

Actually, he was off by two years, but that was absolutely none of his business, and she willed herself again not to react. She didn't want to telegraph to the women in the audience that she cared whether this man found her attractive or not.

"Okay," Nick said. "Twenty-eight it is." His gaze slid down her body, lingering on her legs. "I'm guessing she's got some really nice legs, but underneath the wool pants she's wearing, it's hard to tell. Now, up on top…" He eyed her breasts with such intensity that she had to resist the urge to fold her arms over her chest. "Unfortunately, she left the spandex at home today, and her buttoned-up cotton shirt kinda hinders the view."

"So what score do you give her?" Andy asked.

Nick sighed. "I'm afraid I can't go any higher than a six."

Sara's eyes flew open wide. "A *six?*"

She instantly clamped her mouth shut. *Damn it.* He'd dangled the bait and she'd snapped at it. She'd known exactly what he was up to, and still—

"Wait a minute, Sara," Nick said. "Let me clarify. I'm pretty darned sure there's a ten under there somewhere, but I can't go jumping to conclusions with the obstructed view and all. Now, if you could see your way clear to get rid of some of that cotton and wool, I might be persuaded to reevaluate."

For several seconds, Sara was dumbfounded into silence. Did he seriously think she'd consider such a thing, as if she was one of the strippers he was so famous for interviewing? Was she supposed to take this kind of thing lying down?

Then, out of nowhere, she was hit with an image of taking all kinds of things from Nick Chandler while lying down.

Oh, *God*. Why was her brain going there at a time like this? What was the *matter* with her?

"Never mind, Sara," Nick said. "Numbers really aren't that important, now are they? Let's take a few more calls." He punched a button on the console. "I've got Tawny in Forest Heights on the line. Hey, Tawny. Welcome to the show."

"This question is for Sara," she said.

Sara sat up and squared her shoulders. Finally. A woman who wanted to ask a serious question. She leaned into the microphone. "Yes?"

"I've never seen Nick in person," Tawny said. "Is he as gorgeous as his picture on the Web site?"

Sara flicked her gaze to Nick, who was wearing a smile of supreme satisfaction.

What was she supposed to do now? If she said yes, he'd become so arrogant and unbearable that his ego would ooze right out of this studio. If she said no, her nose would grow like Pinocchio's on steroids. There was only one way to deal with this.

It was time to fight fire with fire.

She took hold of her microphone. "Hi, Tawny. You want to know if Nick is as gorgeous as his picture on the Web site?"

"Oh, yeah."

"Well, maybe it's time for me to do a rundown of my own. Let me tell you what *I'm* looking at."

She turned and stared at Nick, who responded only by leaning back in his chair, folding his arms over his chest and giving her a challenging smile.

"Nick Chandler is the kind of man who makes every woman he meets check her chest for the heart she's sure she's lost. And no wonder. When it comes to good looks, this man went through the line twice. He's got a smile that would light up New York in the middle of a blackout. A body that dropped right down from Mount Olympus. I suspect he's given more than one woman a case of whiplash just by walking past her."

A big grin spread across Nick's face. He leaned into his microphone. "Tawny, I've got to tell you. This woman really knows what she's talking about."

"Hold on, Nick," Sara said. "I'm not finished yet."

"Oh, I'm sorry," he said with a smug smile. "Did I interrupt?"

She leaned into the microphone again. "Given his excessive good looks, I suspect he never developed any real talent because he never had to. That's why he hosts a radio show that relies strictly on his physical attractiveness and his magnetic yet misguided personality. Where women are concerned, he's as full of empty promises as he is of BS. He's the kind of man who wouldn't think to ask 'Was it good for you, too?' because he couldn't fathom that five minutes in his presence wouldn't drive a woman to orgasm. And while you're busy thinking about the future, he's wondering how many beers are left in the fridge.

"So, without demeaning him by asking him to strip to make the assessment, I'd give him a ten-plus for looks. What I'd give him for what's underneath those good looks, though, would be a big fat zero."

A few seconds of dead air passed, and the flicker of amazement on Nick's face gave Sara a rush of vindication. *Yes.* She'd scored a direct hit. Let him try to mess with her after *that*.

To her surprise, though, his expression morphed into a grin of sheer delight. "Well," he said into the microphone, "there may be a little frost on her windows, but it looks as if the furnace inside is going full blast. So how about it, guys? If you like your women feisty, this one might be worth turning off the big screen for. Give me a call and tell me what you think."

As the phone lines lit up, anger rumbled inside Sara like a volcano ready to blow. Feisty? Had he just called her *feisty*? And how had this interview gotten to be about *her,* anyway?

Nick started to touch a button to pick up another call, only to put a finger to his headphones. "Oops. Sorry, guys. Butch is telling me we're out of time." He swung around and grabbed the copy of Sara's book from the table beside him. "The name of the book is *Chasing the Bad Boy,* by Sara Davenport. Buy it because you believe it or buy it because you don't, but whatever you do, buy it. Then drop Sara an e-mail at—" he flipped to the back of the book "—Sara at Sara Davenport dot com and tell her what you think. Now, don't go away. We'll be back in just a few minutes with a little sports talk."

Nick punched a button, then pulled off his headphones and faced her. "Wow, Sara. You really let me have it, didn't you?"

Sara couldn't believe this. As if it was her fault they'd squared off the way they had? He'd baited her, angered her and demeaned her, and now he was upset because she'd given him a dose of his own medicine?

She pulled off her headphones. "Look, Nick. If you're expecting an apology—"

"Apology? Are you kidding? That was what I call damned good radio." He gave her a radiant smile. "Don't let this get out, but I swear sometimes it's better than sex."

Huh?

He leaned toward her, dropping his voice. "How about you, Sara? Did you feel the rush?"

What the *hell* was he talking about? "All I felt," she said hotly, "was the desire to get out of here. You made me look like a fool."

Nick drew back. "Nobody looked like a fool. Least of all you."

"But all those things you said—"

"Yes. I said a lot of things. And you gave them right back to me. We lit up those lines. That's a *good* thing."

"No, it's not," she said, standing up. "Not when you humiliate me to make it happen."

She turned to leave. Nick rose and grabbed her arm. "Hey, take it easy, okay? I don't want you going away mad."

She shook her arm loose and glared at him. "Too late for that."

"Okay," he said, holding up his palms. "I can see that we got off on the wrong foot here."

"You have a talent for understatement."

"So how about we start over?" A smile eased across his face. "Say…with dinner tonight?"

Sara drew back in total disbelief. "You have *got* to be joking."

"I never joke about food. I know a great steakhouse on Campbell Road that's got a rib eye that I just might sell my soul for."

"No, thank you."

He frowned. "Oh, boy. It's the red meat thing, isn't it? Are you one of those women who eats only green stuff?"

"No!"

He sighed with relief. "Thank God. Nothing's worse than taking a vegetarian to a steak house. They end up eating a salad and poking at a baked potato." He smiled again. "So how about it, Sara? Wanna make an evening of it?"

This was absolutely unbelievable. How could he even *think* she'd take him up on such a thing?

"I told you I'm not interested," she said. "And I can't imagine why you would be, either. I mean, why would you want to get stuck with a six like me when you could thumb through your little black book and come up with a perfect ten?"

"Come on, Sara. That rating thing is just a gimmick. My listeners love it."

"Well, I don't."

"Okay, then. Forget the numbers. Here's the truth." He moved closer, his mouth edging into a warm smile. "When you walked in here a few minutes ago, my very first thought was that you were just—quite simply—one *beautiful* woman."

For a moment, she thought she heard a note of actual sincerity in his voice, one that almost made her think he wasn't just tossing compliments around because she'd turned him down and his ego couldn't take it.

Almost.

"No, Nick. *Here's* the truth. Your opinion of my physical appearance doesn't interest me in the least. I was here to promote my book, not to subject myself to your adolescent behavior. But you know what? It's my fault. I knew what your show was like, and I let my publicist book me on it, anyway. But you can bet your life I won't make a mistake like that again."

"Nick!" Butch said. "You got fifteen seconds!"

Nick's smile faded, replaced by a look of resignation. "Okay, Sara. I get the message."

"Good."

She started to walk out.

"Sara?"

"What?"

"If you ever change your mind, you know where to find me."

He put on his headphones and hit a button on the console. As he started his well-practiced banter once again, Sara left the booth, still fuming, still frustrated, and when she thought about the people all over town who had just heard her humiliation, she wanted to crawl under a rock and die.

You know where to find me. As if she'd ever get within a mile of this radio station again.

When she came into the lobby, Karen stood up. Sara brushed past her and headed for the door.

"Hey, wait a minute!" Karen said. "Where are you going? I wanted to meet—"

"No. You don't want to meet him. Trust me. You don't."

She yanked open the door and stepped outside. Traipsing through the snow, she headed for her car, the bitter winter wind swirling around her. Karen threw the strap of her laptop case over her shoulder and followed. She caught up to Sara in the parking lot and pulled her to a halt. "Hey! What's wrong?"

"What's wrong? Did you not hear that interview?"

"I heard every word."

"It was a disaster!"

"Disaster? Are you kidding? You were *brilliant!*"

Sara gaped with disbelief. "Brilliant? What are you talking about? That man humiliated me!"

"No way. He may have given it to you, but you gave it right back. You beat him at his own game."

"No. All I did was let him drag me down into the gutter right along with him."

"Yeah, and while you two were wallowing around in

that gutter, I was checking the e-mails coming in through your Web site. Half a dozen already."

"What?"

"Get in the car. I'll show you."

They slid into the car, and Karen flipped open her laptop. She ran her finger over the touch pad, then tapped.

"Listen to this," she said. "'I just heard you on Nick Chandler's show. You're absolutely right. Somebody needs to warn women about men like him. Keep up the good work!'"

Sara blinked with surprise.

"Here's another one," Karen said. "'I liked how you let him have it. If I had that kind of backbone with a man, then maybe I never would have stayed with the losers I have.'" Karen hit the touch pad again. "And how about this one? 'I came to one of your seminars, and now after hearing you on Nick Chandler's show today, I can see that you're somebody who actually practices what she preaches. You don't let men mess with you. Way to go!'"

Sara was dumbfounded. "They actually heard me? Women who aren't Nick Chandler groupies?"

"If they were before, they're not now. They heard you, they thought about what you said and they responded. And there are more e-mails coming in. Didn't I tell you this would happen?"

Sara felt a glimmer of hope. "I still don't believe it."

"Believe it. You reached your target audience. You may have done it under the radar, but you did it just the same. It appears that Nick Chandler was his own worst enemy in there, and he didn't even know it."

His own worst enemy?

The more Sara thought about that, the more it made sense. He'd baited her into unmasking him just enough that at least a few of the women in his audience had been able to see him for what he really was. And that was a very good thing.

Then all at once, an inkling of an idea came to Sara. She froze, her hands on the steering wheel, as it took shape in her mind. She felt a spark of excitement, which grew hotter with every second that passed.

"Oh, my God. Karen. I know the angle for my next book."

"What?"

"Maybe it's time the women of the world knew exactly what goes on inside the mind of a man like Nick Chandler."

"What do you mean?"

"I wrote my first book from the perspective of women who fall prey to bad boys. What if I write my second one from the perspective of the bad boy himself?"

"Nick?"

"Exactly. He'll be my starting point. Once women have a peek inside his head, see his motives, hear firsthand how he goes about controlling and manipulating them, they'll know he's the kind of man they need to avoid at all cost."

Karen's eyes flicked back and forth, her mind turning. "Sounds promising. PR-wise, it could be a gold mine. But how are you going to get Nick Chandler to spill all his secrets?"

"You said it yourself—he's his own worst enemy. He doesn't see anything wrong with his point of view, and with an ego like his, getting him to talk about himself should be a breeze." She gave her friend a devious smile. "Believe me, Karen. If I want to know what Nick Chandler is thinking, all I have to do is ask."

3

Two hours later, Nick swung his car out of the KZAP parking lot onto the snow-crusted road to head home. Sixteen inches of snow had hit the city already, and more was falling. His windshield wipers were working overtime to sweep enough away that he could see to drive.

He pulled up to a stoplight, then turned to look at Sara Davenport's book lying in the passenger seat beside him. Why he was bringing it home with him, he really didn't know. It had sat on the table beside him during the rest of his show this afternoon, distracting him to the point that he'd actually lost his train of thought a time or two. Finally, he'd stuck it under his desk, thinking *out of sight, out of mind,* only to see Sara's face in his mind instead.

And now the book was staring up at him in that same accusing way it had in the studio. For an inanimate object, it was doing a pretty good job of generating a whole lot of guilt.

He sighed. *Face it, Chandler. You screwed up.*

The minute he'd seen those lines light up during his show, he'd responded as he always did, like some kind of Pavlovian dog with his tail wagging wildly and his mouth watering. As he pictured every one of those incoming lines jammed with callers, his heart had raced and his nerves had come to life, driving him to fan those flames until they burned as hot as they possibly could.

But the more he thought about it, the more he realized that he'd fueled that bonfire at Sara Davenport's expense.

Technically, he'd done things right. He'd entertained his listeners, stirred up a little attention-getting controversy, and plugged her book. Unfortunately, she hadn't exactly gotten into the spirit of his show. And he was still stinging from her turning down his dinner invitation, too, because that meant she was holding a grudge, and he hated that. He'd been a lot of things to a lot of women in his life, but *enemy* had never been one of them.

He hadn't been lying. She *was* a beautiful woman, which made her turning down his dinner invitation doubly painful. He glanced at her book again and let out a heavy sigh. He was going to have to do something to rectify the situation, but he just wasn't sure what.

A few minutes later, he pulled into his parking space next to his apartment and killed the engine, thankful that he'd moved to a new apartment only five minutes from the station. It was bigger than his last one, and the covered parking was a real plus in a city with an average annual snowfall of almost ninety inches. His recent salary increase had afforded him all kinds of luxuries: more space, more comfort, more convenience. All very good things.

Nick grabbed Sara's book, got out of the car and trudged through the snow to his apartment door. Glancing through the window into his living room, he saw a familiar head sticking up above the back of the sofa. He checked his watch. No wonder. He was late getting home tonight, and the game started in ten minutes.

Nick unlocked the door, stomped the snow off his boots and walked inside to find that Ted, as usual, had let himself in and parked himself in front of Nick's big-screen TV, which he said beat the hell out of the piddly twenty-six incher in his own apartment.

"Hey, man!" Ted said. "About time you got home. The game's about to start."

Nick closed the door and tossed Sara's book down on the coffee table. "Let me grab a beer. Need another one?"

"Has the answer to that question ever been no?"

Nick pulled two bottles from the fridge and they sat down on the sofa. Ted looked as he always did, which wasn't surprising since his wardrobe consisted of three pair of jeans and sixty-two concert and radio station T-shirts. And Nick knew that sixteen inches of snow was the only thing on the planet that could make Ted swap his flip-flops for the boots he was wearing now.

He and Ted had met for the first time when Nick had been an intern at KPAT in Colorado Springs. Ted had been their morning man along with another DJ, a guy who was a genius behind the microphone but had a reliability problem stemming from his close personal relationship with the whiskey bottle. When that guy got canned, Ted had lobbied for Nick to fill the spot, telling the station manager that he needed a pretty face to balance his own butt-ugly one because wearing a ski mask during remotes seemed a little too serial killer. It had been an unheard-of opportunity for someone who'd done as little dues-paying as Nick had, and he vowed he'd never forget it.

They'd been a great team on a show with great ratings, but eventually they'd been fired. Nick figured that the hoax they'd pulled on the mayor probably had something to do with it. They'd split up, Ted heading to Monroe, Louisiana, and Nick to Dallas, then Chicago, before finally landing in Boulder. Nick had learned his lesson. He kept the practical jokes to a minimum, stayed put and built a reputation, finally working his way up to his own show. Ted hopped from job to job, eventually ending up at a low-watt hole-in-the-wall FM station in Tupelo.

When he'd called three months ago to tell Nick that he'd been fired one more time, Nick hadn't been surprised. There was always some stunt Ted wanted to pull, music he declined to play, or ass he refused to kiss. But this time Nick had heard a touch of desperation in his friend's voice that had never been there before, so he pulled a few strings and got him an interview for a producer's job at KZAP. At first, Ted had flipped out: *I've been playing rock and roll across this great country of ours for the past twenty years, and you want me to produce a gardening show?* But then he'd gotten real and gotten down to business, taking the job when it was offered and staying with Nick until he could get back on his feet again.

"Caught your show today," Ted said. "Great stuff. Loved Amber, the pole dancing champion." He drooped his lids and assumed a Madonna-like voice. "'It's, like, you have to become one with the pole. Feel the pole. *Love* the pole.'"

"Hey, everybody's got their thing. I respect that." Nick gave him a sly grin. "Her thing just happens to be slithering naked up and down a pole in front of a roomful of drunk men."

And after her spot on the show, Amber had offered to show Nick the practice pole in her bedroom, complete with a private performance. When he'd declined, she'd given him an open invitation for the future. In light of Amber's considerable physical assets, he'd surprised himself by feeling more turned off by her than turned on.

Then Sara Davenport had shown up.

He'd looked around to see her standing at the door of the

studio, uptight and buttoned-down, but still considerably sexier than any psychologist he'd ever imagined. The nervousness she'd tried to hide had only made him wonder what other chinks there might be in the armor of rigid professionalism she wore. Only seconds passed before he was already thinking about pulling those glasses off her real slow, tossing them aside, then taking her in his arms and...

"But your best bit was that psychologist," Ted said. "She really let you have it, didn't she? God, that was *great*. The kind of guest you kill for."

"Yeah, I know. Unfortunately, the lady didn't think it was all that entertaining. She thought I humiliated her."

"You kidding? She got her shots in, didn't she?"

"Yeah, but she still didn't think much of me by the time the interview was over. I tried to ask her out to dinner as a peace offering, but that didn't fly, either."

"Are you telling me a woman turned you down?"

"It's hardly the first time."

"Yeah, but it's the first time since you were twelve years old." He reached to the coffee table. "Is this her book?"

"Yeah."

Ted thumbed through it. "Wow. Check out her bio. Education out the wazoo." He turned to Nick. "Since when do you have a thing for the intellectual type?"

He didn't. At least, he didn't think he did.

Did he?

"I just didn't want her to go away mad," Nick said. "That's bad for business."

"So which was she? A six or a ten?"

Nick winced. He'd taken that bit a little too far. Sara wasn't a mud wrestler or a *Penthouse* pet or the owner of a nudist resort. Those women were used to his kind of banter. They *thrived* on his kind of banter.

Sara didn't.

"That's just a stupid bit I do," Nick said. "I'm thinking of trashing it."

"No way. It's that kind of bit that got you where you are. That show's a cash cow, kid. Milk it for all it's worth. If you don't, one of these days you'll be old and decrepit like me, and you won't be good for much of anything." He took a swig of beer. "Well, anything except producing a *gardening* show."

"For God's sake, Ted. You're only forty-one."

"In radio, I might as well be a hundred and forty-one." He pointed his finger at Nick. "Take this as a warning, kid. This business chews you up and spits you out." Then he waved his hand dismissively. "Oh, hell, why am I warning you? You're riding the wave. If they're talking syndication for your show, you're gonna be on easy street."

"They're talking. But I'm not holding my breath."

"Nope. You've got what it takes. I knew it from the second I met you. Syndication will put you on top, so you do anything—and I mean *anything*—to get there. You hear me? Otherwise you're gonna end up like me in ten years. Look how I was wallowing around at the bottom of the barrel when I called you a few months ago."

"You were out of a job. Like that's something new to radio guys?"

To Nick's surprise, Ted's expression turned solemn, and he stared down at his beer. "You know, when I got fired, I was at the end of my rope. I wasn't quite sure where I was gonna go. I just hung around Tupelo for a few days, staring at the wall. Then I talked to you." He turned his gaze up to meet Nick's. "Thanks, kid. I don't know what I'd have done without you."

Nick's heart twisted a little. "Hey, it was purely selfish on my part, believe me."

"How's that?"

"At the rate I'm going, I'm never going to have a wife, but what do I need one of those for when I have you waiting for me when I get home? If I could just get you to have dinner ready and bring me my slippers, I'd be all set."

Ted scowled. "Hey, you know the number of the pizza place as well as I do. And your big stinky feet can freeze for all I care. Now, just watch the game, will you?"

Nick grinned and picked up the remote, when all at once the phone rang. He tossed the remote aside and grabbed it.

"This is Nick."

"Hi, Nick. This is Sara Davenport."

His heart skipped. Hers was the last voice he'd expected to hear on the other end of the line, and for a moment he was actually speechless.

"Did I catch you at a bad time?" she asked.

"Uh, no," he said, sitting up straight. "Not at all. I'm just…well, I guess I'm a little surprised. I didn't expect to hear from you again."

"I phoned the station and your producer gave me your home number. I hope you don't mind."

"Of course not." Nick's mind was spinning, wondering why she was calling. "I just hope this means you've reconsidered my dinner invitation."

"No," she said. "I'm not calling about dinner. But there is something I'd like to discuss with you. A business proposition."

Business? He could think of all kinds of business he'd like to get down to with her. Unfortunately, she sounded as if she meant, well…*business.*

"Can you meet me at my office tomorrow at ten o'clock?"

Nick ran through his mental to-do list for tomorrow and saw nothing on his schedule for that hour. And between now and then, if he remembered something, he'd cancel it.

"Sure, Sara. I can meet you at ten."

"Good. My office address is 8442 Cavanaugh Court, Suite 214."

Nick grabbed a pencil and scribbled the address on the cover of his *TV Guide*. "Care to tell me what we're gonna be talking about?"

"I'd rather go into it tomorrow, if you don't mind."

"Sure. That's fine."

"I'll see you then."

"I'll be looking forward to it."

Nick heard a click. He held out the phone and stared at it for a moment, then turned to Ted. "That's weird."

"What?"

He returned the phone to its cradle. "That was Sara Davenport."

"The shrink on the show today?"

"Yeah. She wants me to meet her at her office tomorrow morning."

Ted raised his eyebrows. "Her office, huh? Why there?"

"I don't know. She's says it's business."

Ted grinned. "Business? Right. Don't psychologists have couches in their offices?"

"They do on TV."

"Well, there you go, kid."

"What?"

"I'd say she's looking for a little afternoon delight. This way, you don't even have to buy her dinner."

"Will you give me a break? It's nothing like that. Trust me.

When she left the station, she was cold as ice. And I don't sense that a whole lot of thawing has taken place since then."

"Oh, yeah? Bet you can lock her office door, draw the blinds and get her naked in under two minutes."

Nick gave him a deadpan stare. "Ted?"

"Yeah?"

"You really need to get a love life of your own."

"Nah. What woman in her right mind is gonna want a washed-up bum like me? Just hand me a beer and let me live vicariously."

As Ted picked up the remote and found the station the game was on, Nick glanced at the phone again, still wondering why Sara wanted to see him.

And why he wanted to see her.

It was crazy, after all. Sara wasn't anything like the kind of women he usually dated. She'd probably never done a Jell-O shot in her life. Or picked up a pool cue. Or flashed her boobs during Mardi Gras, worn a thong or woken up in Cancun with a hangover and wondered how she'd gotten there. Instead, she'd been busy getting all those letters after her name and writing books, not to mention straightening out people's minds and collecting a hefty paycheck for her services. Just being seen with a sharp, conservative, intellectual woman like Sara would make his bar-hopping, speed-dating, sports-crazy listeners wonder when he'd gone over to the dark side.

So why did he feel a hot little rush at the very thought of seeing her again?

He had no idea. He only knew that it had been a very long time since he'd met a woman who was any kind of challenge at all. Most of the women he encountered were either waiting in the lobby of the station to slip their phone numbers into his pocket, calling his show with various sexual propositions or tossing their panties into the booth whenever he did remotes. He tried to imagine Sara doing any of those things, and he almost laughed out loud.

He settled back with Ted to watch the game, but he had a hard time concentrating. Business? He had no idea if Sara ever mixed that with pleasure, but he sure intended to find out.

4

"NICK CHANDLER is coming *here?*"

Sara's assistant stared at her with big brown eyes full of rapt disbelief, more proof that Nick's notoriety was even more widespread than Sara had imagined.

She closed the folder she held and strode to the file cabinet. "Yes, Heather. He'll be here in just a few minutes."

"I can't believe it," Heather said. "I just can't *believe* it. I mean, I saw the name on your schedule, but I had no idea it was *the* Nick Chandler. What's the deal? Is he really messed up or crazy or something?"

"Heather, we don't say crazy," Sara said, refiling the folder. "Haven't we talked about that?"

"Oh, yeah. I'm sorry. I'll be careful not to say that to his face. I promise."

"It's a good idea to get used to not saying it behind somebody's back, either."

Heather nodded dutifully.

"And he's not a client. We just have some business to discuss." She glanced at Heather's desk. "Did you get the filing done?"

"Yeah. And all of it's in the right place, too."

Sara smiled. "Good job."

When Sara hired Heather two months ago, it had been like rescuing a homeless puppy from a snowstorm, minus the wet fur, the cold nose and the peeing on the rug. But the job wasn't that demanding, and Sara had felt sorry for her. Like that little lost puppy, turning her away had been next to impossible.

Still, in spite of the fact that Heather truly needed a job, when she continued to cut clients off on the phone and misfile important documents, Sara had told her that perhaps this wasn't the job for her. But as soon as Heather saw the ax falling, those big brown eyes had filled with tears. Then, like the Hoover Dam bursting and flooding half of Arizona, Heather had unloaded her entire employment history on Sara.

I broke the copier at that law firm and I spilled coffee on the chairman of the board at that manufacturing company and then there was that grease fire I started at McDonald's when I was seventeen and ohmiGod I just know this means I'll never be able to find a job again…

Sara had never thought of herself as a pushover, but suddenly she just couldn't fire her. Heather had a two-year degree and wasn't lacking in intellect. She was just painfully naive and woefully unsure of herself. Once firing her had been taken off the table, Sara was left with no option but to let her grow into the job. And day by day, she was doing better.

"And you'll be proud of me for something else," Heather said.

"What's that?"

"I'm going to break up with Richard tonight."

Sara's heart skipped with hope. Heather had read Sara's book, and after they'd talked about it, slowly she'd come to the conclusion that her boyfriend fit a lot of the criteria for the kind of man she needed to stay away from. Their relationship had been one of him promising her the moon and giving her nothing at the same time he couldn't keep his hands off other women.

"I think you're doing the right thing," Sara said.

Heather sighed. "I hope so."

"He's going to try to manipulate you again. You just have to be ready for that."

"I know. I'm sticking to my guns this time. I swear I am."

Sara smiled. "Good for you."

With Christmas only a week from tomorrow, Sara was proud of Heather for taking this initiative right now. Making such a decision was especially hard around the holidays, when emotions ran high and resistance ran low. Sara herself had gotten a little flustered when Nick had interviewed her yesterday, so she knew how easy it was to succumb to the manipulation of a man like Heather's boyfriend. Of course, now that she had a little distance on the experience and had had time to analyze her reaction, she was in control now. He wouldn't be getting to her again. And she felt absolutely certain of that, right up to the moment when the door swung open and Nick walked into the office and her heart went crazy all over again.

He was dressed similarly to the way he was yesterday, only the sweater was a different color, and he wore a fleece-lined leather coat over it. He suddenly seemed taller. Bigger. She told herself it was just the coat, or maybe his boots, or…

Or maybe it was his larger-than-life personality that was oozing right off him, which included a smile so bright it could be seen from outer space.

"Hello, Nick," she said, striving for nonchalance. "Come in."

Heather, however, didn't know the meaning of the word *nonchalance*, staring at Nick as if the untouchable dream man from her deepest fantasies had just come to life in front of her. And her thunderstruck expression wasn't lost on Nick.

"Hi, there," he said, turning that Day-Glo smile full force in her direction. "I'm Nick Chandler."

Heather just looked at him as if her brain had shut down completely. And Sara had the most terrible feeling that she had an even dumber look on her own face.

But why? *Why?* He was just one man.

Okay, he was just one *highly attractive* man, but she knew what was beneath the surface. And she intended never to forget that, no matter how charming he seemed to be.

"Nick, this is my assistant, Heather."

"Very nice to meet you, Heather," Nick said.

"My boyfriend listens to your show all the time," she gushed. "He just loves it." Then she glanced quickly at Sara, her smile fading. "I mean, my *ex*-boyfriend."

"Heather," Sara said, "will you please hold my calls while Mr. Chandler and I talk?"

Nick gave Heather a little wink as they walked away, and Sara thought the poor girl was going to melt right there.

Once they were in her office, Sara closed the door behind them and sat down in the chair behind her desk. Nick took off his coat and tossed it onto one of her guest seats. He circled his gaze around the room.

"Nice office, Sara. Or should I call you Dr. Davenport? With this big old desk between us, I feel like maybe I ought to."

"No, Sara will be fine."

He walked over to her bookshelves and scanned the titles. "Hmm. No Freud? No Jung?" He turned back with a smile. "What kind of a psychologist are you, anyway?"

"Have a seat, Nick."

"Hold on," he said, glancing at her diplomas hanging

on the wall. "Gotta check out the credentials." He looked at them, then gave her a low whistle of approval. "Wow. Are you sure you're only twenty-eight?"

"I'm thirty."

He grinned. "Ah. Fibbed a little about your age, did you?"

"No. You said twenty-eight. I didn't correct you."

"Don't worry," he said with a grin. "Your secret is safe with me."

"It's no secret."

"Uh-huh." He moved to the window and opened the blinds. "Great view of the mountains. The windows at the station look out onto parking lots and Dumpsters." He sighed wistfully. "I knew I should have majored in psychology."

"Nick? Can we talk?"

"Oh, yeah. Right. Business."

He sat down in the chair in front of her desk, crossing one ankle casually over his knee and placing his elbows on the arms of the chair. With his fingers steepled in front of him, he lounged there as if he belonged there. She had a feeling that no matter where this man went, he instantly made himself at home.

"Okay, Sara. Shoot."

She sat up straight, choosing her words carefully. "As you know, I've written one book. Now I'm in the process of writing another one."

"Yes?"

"And I'm interested in your point of view."

"My point of view? About what?"

"Well, my new book is going to contain the same kind of subject matter as my last one, but with a twist. I'm interested in investigating the subject from a man's perspective. You seem to have strong opinions about man-woman relationships, so I thought it would be interesting to quote you."

Suddenly the man who'd been bouncing all over her office went completely still, his cheery expression fading away. His eyes narrowed into a stare so intense that she had the sensation of being completely transparent.

"I didn't think you were overly fond of my opinions."

"The most thorough examination of any issue encompasses more than one point of view."

"Even though mine is the wrong one?"

"Your words will speak for themselves."

"True, but I won't have any control over the spin you do in the next paragraph, will I?"

"I can only promise to quote you accurately. If you stand by your opinions, and those opinions are shared by your audience members, then any spin I do shouldn't make a difference, should it?"

He was silent for a long time. Staring at her. Staring *into* her. His eyes were narrowed, his gaze locked on to hers. She forced herself not to look away. For a moment, she was sure he was going to say no. Then his tense posture seemed to relax, and a tiny smile crossed his lips.

"Sure, Sara," he said. "I'd be happy to give you my point of view."

Sara felt a rush of relief. "Good. That's good." She reached for her planner. "We can set a time for you to come back here and—"

"Nope. I don't want to talk here. As I said, I'm not real crazy about this big old desk between us."

"If you'd prefer, we can sit on the sofa."

He examined it for a moment. "Well, I admit that's a step in the right direction, but..." He turned back. "No. I don't think so."

"Then where do you suggest we do the interview?"

"Over dinner."

Her heart kicked up a notch. "Dinner?"

"Yeah. Good food and good wine make everything so much more enjoyable, don't you think?"

She should have known this wasn't going to be as easy as it appeared. *Nothing* with this man was as easy as it appeared.

"Didn't I tell you yesterday that I'm not interested in going out with you?"

"That was yesterday. This is today."

"Nothing's changed."

"If it makes you feel better, think of it as a business dinner."

No. No way. She had to be firm with him, or he was going to run all over her.

"I'm sorry, Nick. Any interview I conduct is going to take place right here."

"Is that your final word on the subject?"

"Yes. It is."

"Then the deal's off."

He rose from his chair, grabbed his coat and headed for the door.

Sara stood up suddenly. "Wait!"

Slowly he turned back.

She sighed with frustration. "I don't understand why you're being difficult about this. There's no good reason—"

"On the contrary. There's a very good reason I'm being difficult."

"Which is?"

He spoke slowly and distinctly. "Because I want to have dinner with you."

"Why?"

"Why? Well, let's see. It's this little ritual men and women sometimes perform. It's called a date."

"You told me to think of it as a business dinner!"

"Right. You think of it as a business dinner. I'll think of it as a date."

"Then we'd be at cross-purposes, wouldn't we?"

"Isn't your goal to find out how a man like me thinks?"

"Yes."

"Believe me, Sara. By the end of the evening, you'll know *exactly* what's on my mind."

A shiver of awareness crept up Sara's spine, clashing wildly with the warning bells sounding inside her head. She knew this was nothing but a power play, but still she couldn't stop the gut-level reaction that came from listening to a very sexy man alluding to very sexy things.

"Can I ask you a question?" Nick said.

"Yes?"

"You seem pretty wrapped up in your work. When was the last time you went on a date?"

Sara felt a start of self-consciousness. "That's none of your business."

"In other words, you'd have to look at last year's calendar?"

"My personal life has nothing to do with this."

"Good God. Has it been *two* years?"

"Of course it hasn't!"

He shook his head sadly. "You work too hard."

"My career is important to me."

"So is mine, but I still find time to have fun."

"Your career is based on nothing *but* having fun."

"Which means I'm an expert at it." He flashed her another one of those warm, engaging smiles. "Stick with me, Sara, and I'll show you how it's done."

For just a moment, that smile put her on the verge of letting down her guard. Then she thought about how he'd smiled at her this same way yesterday, too, right before he humiliated her in front of a hundred thousand people.

Still, what could it hurt to spend the evening with him? They'd be in a public place, so it wasn't as if he could make a move on her right there at the table. And in the meantime, she'd be getting what she wanted from him. The more she thought about it, the more she realized that she really had nothing to lose.

"Yes, Nick. All right. I'll go to dinner with you."

"Great. How about tomorrow night at seven?"

"Fine. Where do you want me to meet you?"

"We'll go to Luigi's," he said. "Ever been there?"

"No."

"Nice place. Cozy. Quiet." He smiled. "Just right for all that *talking* we're going to do."

Talking. Exactly. With her sitting on one side of the table and him on the other. *Period.*

"But I still don't get this," Sara said. "I haven't made a secret of the fact that I think men like you are bad for women. So why in the world do you want to have dinner with me?"

"Because I'd like the chance to change your mind about that."

"It's unlikely that's going to happen."

"Now, Sara," he said, giving her a knowing smile. "You of all people should know that you should never underestimate a man like me."

With that, he slipped out the door and closed it behind him. For several seconds, Sara just stood there, feeling the aura of sexual energy he left in his wake.

Good Lord. What had she just agreed to?

She'd gotten what she wanted. An interview with Nick Chandler. But now that businesslike discussion she'd envisioned had just become an intimate Italian dinner at a cozy little restaurant. She knew manipulation was his middle name. So why had she let him get away with that?

It didn't matter. They'd be in a public place. And if she was the smart, educated woman with high self-esteem she'd always professed to be, of course she could hold her own with a man like him. If she couldn't, she had no business telling other women how to do it.

But the truth was that Nick wasn't really interested in her. She'd just bruised his ego yesterday when she'd rejected him, and this was his way of regaining power. It was classic bad-boy behavior. Predictable as clockwork.

And as long as she remembered that, she was going to have no problem with him at all.

5

THE NEXT DAY at noon, Nick found himself sitting at a table in just the kind of trendy restaurant he hated. At places like this one, the decor was weird, the waiters were snotty and the menu items were so unrecognizable he was never quite sure what he was eating. And to get charged a premium price for the privilege of being left in the dark really added insult to injury.

But today he wasn't picking up the tab. That honor fell to his agent, Mitzi Grant, who had taken him to lunch to fill him in on her ongoing negotiations with Mercury Media. Mitzi was forty-six years old and barely five feet tall, fast-talking and sharp-dressing, a tiny little package of dynamite who was arguably one of the best entertainment agents in the country. Nick had learned to overlook the fact that she was also blunt and pushy and demanding, because her record spoke for itself. With Mitzi on his side, he had a good shot at hitting the big time.

Mitzi grabbed the last of some raw fish appetizer from her plate with a practiced flick of her chopsticks. The food here was supposed to be something called Asian fusion. Nick wasn't sure exactly what was being fused to what, but right now a T-bone fused with a little steak sauce would look pretty good to him.

"Things are right on track," Mitzi told him. "I'd say we

could be looking at a syndication contract by the first of the year."

"You're talking like it's a done deal."

"You're hot, Nick. You've got that nice little blend of charm and audacity that your listeners thrive on. The Mercury people are making all the right noises, and I'm starting to think that it's not so much a matter of a contract coming together as it is how much money I can squeeze out of them."

Nick felt a surge of excitement. This was something he'd wanted for years, and he couldn't believe it was on the verge of happening.

"They like your attitude," Mitzi said. "And they like the outrageous stuff you do, like when you interviewed the ex-madam. And the singing sex therapist. Oh—and they also mentioned that interview you did with the psychologist." She gave him a sly smile. "That was pure gold."

Yeah, he'd been on target that day, all right. And Sara hadn't appreciated it in the least.

"Oh," Mitzi said. "Did you see Raycine Clark's column yesterday?"

"No," Nick said warily. "Why?"

Mitzi pulled a folded newspaper from her purse and laid it in front of him. "She seems to think you and Sara Davenport would make quite a couple."

Nick scanned the column.

Yesterday on his radio show, Nick Chandler went toe-to-toe with the ultimate good girl: Sara Davenport, author of the book *Chasing the Bad Boy*. She teaches women how to avoid heartbreakers like Nick, and their opposing opinions made sparks fly. But opposites do attract, and knowing Nick

Chandler, I'm betting that sparks flew between them off the air as well as on.

Nick sighed. There wasn't much he hated more than being in Raycine's sights. Unfortunately, the general population thrived on the gossip she spread in her newspaper column, and she thrived on digging it up.

He tossed down the paper. "What the hell drove her to this conclusion?"

"Don't gripe. It's publicity."

"I mean, I am having dinner with Sara, but—"

"You're having dinner with her?"

When Nick saw Mitzi's calculating stare, he cringed, thinking maybe he should have kept his mouth shut. Mitzi was positively vulturine when it came to promo ops, and he sensed her circling now.

"It's not what you think. I interviewed her, and now she wants to interview me. We're getting together tonight."

"Interview you? What for?"

"For her next book."

Mitzi's dark brows drew together as she processed that information. "Oh, yeah? She tells women how to stay away from guys like you."

"She says she wants the male point of view."

Mitzi looked confused for a moment longer, and then Nick saw the lightbulb go on over her head.

"Ah," she said. "Your male point in view in particular?"

"Yes."

"She wants to quote you, name and all?"

"Uh-huh."

"Then she wants to contradict everything you say?"

"That's a strong possibility."

Mitzi gave him an evil grin. "That's perfect. Pour on the

charm, but be outrageous. Say stuff she can't wait to quote."

"Mitzi—"

"Play it up on your show this afternoon. Tell your listeners that you must have made a real impression on the stuffy shrink, because she wants to quote you in her new book as the ultimate bad boy. They'll eat that up." She grinned. "So will Raycine Clark."

"I'm not sure I want to talk about this on the air."

Mitzi gaped at him. "Nick, sweetie? Are you feeling sick? Losing your edge? When that woman was on your show, you told me those lines lit up like Rio during Carnivale. Now you've got the opportunity to fan those flames all over again. Hell, *yes*, you should talk about this on the air!"

"I think I'd just as soon let this one drop."

"Are you nuts? Sara Davenport is characterizing you as a man who's so magnetic to women that a psychologist has to counsel them on how to resist him, and you want to let that *drop?*"

When he didn't respond, she leaned in closer. "Do I need to remind you of what's at stake right now? The big boys will be buying your image. The more you bolster it, the better you'll look."

"But it might not be so good for Sara."

"Not good? Will you wake *up?* She's got a book out there. Every time you say her name on the air, it's free publicity for her. Why in the hell would anyone object to that?"

Mitzi had a point. It *was* good publicity for her. But he just wasn't sure that Sara would see it that way.

"Hey," Mitzi said, those brows drawing together again. "What's with this sudden concern with Sara Davenport? Huh? Don't tell me you really do have the hots for her."

His heart skipped a little. "No, Mitzi. I don't have the hots for her."

"Well, I didn't think so. She's not your type."

And that was exactly why he wondered why Sara interested him so much. Everything about her office was just as he had predicted it would be. Big cherrywood desk. Fancy art. Draperies and rugs and bookshelves and computer hardware that said, *I'm rich, I'm successful and I haven't had fun since I was ten years old.*

And then there had been Sara herself, dressed in a silk blouse that showed not nearly enough cleavage and a skirt that showed not nearly enough leg. Add a piece or two of silver jewelry and her hair in a twist at the back of her head, and she was a regular poster girl for stuffy professionalism.

He supposed if he were a client of hers, her sharp, competent appearance would give him confidence that she could hop inside his head and flush out a few cobwebs. But since his head was pretty tidy already, all her pristine appearance did was give him the urge to mess it up. He'd wanted to take that hair down and run his fingers through it. Watch that painfully wrinkle-free skirt and blouse hit the floor. Find out if her bra and panties were as utilitarian as everything else she wore.

Then again, when her underwear was lying on the floor with the rest of her clothes, did it really matter?

"You are planning on being at the station's party on New Year's Eve, right?" Mitzi asked.

"Yeah. I'll be there."

"So will I. And so will Dennis Rayburn and his entourage."

Nick came to attention. "The Mercury people are going to be there?"

"Yes. It'll be a good time for a little schmoozing. And since the station is going high-class with this one, you need to rent a tux."

Nick winced. "I can't get away with just a suit?"

"Nope. It's black tie. And you might consider actually buying a tux. It's the uniform of the rich and famous."

And that was probably one of the few things that would make him reconsider wanting to be rich and famous.

The waiter brought their main courses. As they ate, Mitzi reminded Nick between bites that he was to go on his show this afternoon and stir things up all over again. And by the time their lunch was over, Nick had to admit that she was probably right. He needed to use this to his advantage. After all, what harm could it do to tell his listeners that he was having dinner with Sara? Every time he mentioned her name, it was worth a few advertising dollars, promo she was getting absolutely free. And she was using him, too, wasn't she? If she could mention him in her book, he could mention her on the air.

But in the end, Sara interested him not because she made such a good talking point on his show. He'd lied to Mitzi, plain and simple. Against all odds, he did have the hots for Sara Davenport. He hadn't counted on getting the opportunity to spend an evening with her, and he intended to see just how far something between them could go.

AT TWENTY TO SEVEN that evening, Sara tucked one last pin in her hair, then strode into her living room, where Karen sat on the sofa drinking a beer. Sara had checked out the restaurant where Nick had asked her to meet him. Not surprisingly, the dress was very informal, so she'd put on jeans and a casual shirt to avoid looking out of place. She stopped in front of a mirror, pulled lipstick out of her purse and talked as she dabbed.

"I don't mind telling you, Karen. I'm a little nervous about this. If I was meeting Nick at my office, no big deal. But now that we're going to a restaurant, I'm not so sure."

"Actually, you're better off in a public place," Karen said. "In your office, he'd lock the door and have you naked on your sofa before you knew what hit you."

Sara turned to glare at Karen. "Why, thank you for that vote of confidence."

"Oh, come on, Sara. You can handle Nick Chandler and you know it. Just eat, ask your questions and leave. No big deal. Did you hear his show today?"

Sara tucked the lipstick back into her purse. "Sorry. I'm not one of his regular listeners."

"He told them he was having dinner with you."

Sara spun around. "He *what?*"

"Will you get that panic-stricken look off your face? Nick is giving you what amounts to advance publicity for your next book. And then when it comes out, he'll be talking it up like crazy, just like he talked about you today."

"What did he say?"

"Well, let's see. He told them you wanted to interview him for your new book because you'd recognized that he was, after all, an expert on the male point of view. Then he mentioned that although you're a touch on the conservative side, you really are very attractive."

Sara's heart skipped. "He said that?"

"Oh, yeah. And then some guy called in and said he didn't care if a woman looked like a linebacker as long as she could make a decent sandwich and shut up during the game."

"Oh, that's charming."

"Then Nick said he could tell that the guy was a new

listener to the show, because he clearly didn't understand the proper order of things."

"Which is?"

"Women first, sports second."

"Well, thank God for that."

"Except, of course, during the Super Bowl. And the NCAA playoffs. And the Masters Tournament. And the Stanley Cup, as long as it's an American team playing."

Sara closed her eyes. "This is the man I'm having dinner with?"

"This is the man you're interviewing for your book, who has a hundred thousand listeners who'd probably buy a roll of toilet paper if Charmin decided to quote him on the package. He's handing you book sales on a silver platter. And word on the street is that he's heading for syndication. If that happens, so much the better."

Karen had a point. Okay. All she had to do was get through this evening, let Nick reveal himself with all his suggestive banter and crass come-ons, and then she'd leave the restaurant and that would be that.

"They all assume he's out to nail you, of course."

"Oh, that's a lovely way to put it."

Karen smiled. "I think they're right. If he's insisting on having dinner with you, he's probably *very* interested."

"Nick Chandler chases after any woman with a pulse. Where I'm concerned, he only wants what he can't have."

"Are you sure he can't have it?"

"Think, Karen. You're my publicist. What would it do to my credibility to have a relationship with a man like him?"

"Yeah, okay. So forget the relationship. Just hold it to a few secret nights of hot, sweaty sex."

"Secret? Are you kidding? If I go to bed with that man, the entire city of Boulder will get a play-by-play the next day."

"I know you, Sara. The odds of you succumbing to Nick Chandler…hmm. Is it possible for odds to be less than zero?"

Just then her doorbell rang. She went to her front door, looked out the peephole, and her heart froze.

"Oh, God," she moaned. "He's here."

"Who?"

"Nick Chandler."

"What?"

"He's outside right now."

"So answer the door."

"But he's not supposed to be picking me up!"

"You also don't want him turning into a Popsicle. The wind chill out there is ten below."

Sara took a deep, cleansing breath and opened the door. Nick stood on her porch, snow sprinkled on his shoulders, his cheeks red from the cold. He held a big paper bag.

"Nick, why are you here? We were going to meet at the restaurant."

"Small problem with that. Mind if I come in? It's a little bit cold out here."

She opened the door wide and he slipped inside, followed by a gust of frigid air. He pulled off his stocking cap and stuffed it into his pocket. His dark hair was mussed, and he ran his fingers through it, which did little to tame it. The thought actually crossed her mind that the man's messy hair was sexy. What in the hell was the matter with her?

"So what's the problem with going to the restaurant?"

"Luigi called me to let me know that some of my more rabid listeners have been camping out in the bar for the past hour, waiting for us to show up."

"You told them where we were going?"

"Nope. But it's no secret to them what my favorite restaurant is. They were just assuming. And I made a few assumptions myself."

"What assumptions?"

"I assumed that you wouldn't want to conduct an interview with a bunch of rowdy people listening in. And," he said, holding up the sack, "I assumed you like lasagna. I slipped in the back door and had Luigi pack up some takeout."

"We could have gone to another restaurant."

"Nope. I promised my taste buds Luigi's lasagna. They don't like it when I lie to them."

"Sara loves lasagna," Karen said, rising from the sofa. "She gripes about it all going straight to her hips, but she likes it just the same."

Nick turned as she approached. "Have we met? I'm Nick Chandler."

"I'm Karen Dawson, Sara's publicist."

Nick shook Karen's hand, giving her one of those broad, brilliant smiles that turned women to mush, and Karen was already getting a little soft around the edges.

"You're the one who arranged for me to interview Sara," he said.

"Yes," Karen said slyly. "I thought the two of you would really hit it off."

"Oh, we did. We're having dinner together tonight, aren't we?"

"Nick," Sara said sharply. "I told you before. This isn't a date. This is business."

"You know," Nick whispered to Karen, "she keeps saying that, but it's looking more like a date all the time."

Karen had the nerve to smile at that. "Well, in that case, I guess I'd better leave you two alone. You have fun now, you hear?"

"Don't go," Sara said. "I'm sure Nick brought plenty of food for three."

"Sara, don't you dare tempt me like that. You know I'm on a diet and lasagna is out of the question. Give me a call tomorrow, okay?" She tossed on her coat and as she slipped out the door, she gave Sara a suggestive wink. Sara wanted to kill her.

She closed the door, intending to tell Nick that maybe it would be a good idea to reschedule the interview, but he was already heading to her kitchen. He set the sack down on the counter and removed foam boxes from it, once again making himself right at home. And to her surprise, food wasn't all he was taking out. There was also a bottle of wine. And a candle. And then he was pulling out…a tablecloth?

"What's all that?" she asked.

He went to her dining room table, scooted her center-piece aside, then shook out the tablecloth with a snap and let it float to the tabletop. "We couldn't go to the restaurant, so I brought a little of the restaurant here. After all, what's a romantic Italian dinner without a red checkered tablecloth, wine and candlelight?"

"Nick. Listen carefully. *This is not a date.* And that's the last time I'm going to say that!"

"Well, thank God. I knew you'd get tired of protesting sooner or later. Where are your wineglasses?"

This man was impossible.

Okay. What to do now? She could fight it, or she could go through the motions and get the evening over with. Unfortunately, something told her that where Nick was concerned, the second route might be the more expeditious one to take.

She went into the kitchen and took down a pair of wine-glasses. He poked his head into the kitchen.

"Matches?"

"I don't have any."

"Don't lie. You have other candles around the house that you obviously light occasionally, particularly at this time of year."

With a sigh of frustration, she pulled open the drawer to the left of the stove and handed him a box of matches. As she brought the food to the table, he proceeded not only to light the candle he'd brought, but every other one in the living room and dining room. Then she came out of the kitchen with plates and silverware to find him twisting the knob on the dimmer switch and bringing down the lights.

Sara stopped short. "Will you cut that out?"

She deposited the plates and silverware on the table. On her way back to the kitchen to grab napkins, she turned the lights up. When she returned, they were dim again, only this time the knob on the dimmer switch had disappeared.

She glared at him. "All right, Nick. What did you do with the knob?"

He blinked innocently. "What knob?"

She tossed the napkins onto the table with a breath of disgust. "Never mind. Let's just get this over with."

"Oh, no, Sara. Food like this isn't something you hurry through. You have to savor every bite."

Nick pulled out her chair for her, then sat down adjacent to her, so close she felt his knee brush against hers. She scooted away, but still he was way too close for comfort.

As they filled their plates, in spite of the situation, Sara had to admit that the atmosphere looked nice. The food looked good.

And so did Nick.

The candlelight mingling with the glow of the tiny

white lights on her Christmas tree made him look even more handsome than usual, softening his features until his face was positively mesmerizing. As he uncorked the wine, suddenly she realized she was living a scenario that sometimes ran through her mind when she least expected it: a nice evening at home with good food, good wine and a relaxed atmosphere, complete with a warm, engaging, attentive man to share it with…

Stop it. He's not that man, no matter how great he looks. He's up to no good. Never forget that.

She picked up her fork. "Eat fast," she said. "We have an interview to attend to."

He poured her a glass of wine. "Drink slow," he said with a smile. "We've got all night."

6

During dinner, Nick talked about all kinds of things, from the TV shows he watched to the movies he'd seen to the people he knew, all the while trying to drag Sara into a datelike conversation. But she refused to act as if that was what was happening, no matter how much of a romantic atmosphere he'd managed to create on short notice. Maybe he was used to women twirling their hair and staring at him adoringly, but she wasn't going to be one of them.

After they finished dinner, Nick filled their wineglasses again and set them on the coffee table. Sara had no intention of drinking another drop and told him so, but he did it just the same.

As they moved toward the sofa, Sara deliberately sat down near the center of it, so when he did what she expected and sat down too close to her, she had room to shift in the other direction.

"I gotta tell you," Nick said, settling comfortably on the sofa, "I'm a little uptight here. See, I'm at a bit of a disadvantage with a highly intelligent woman like you. You could have me saying all kinds of incriminating things and I'd never know what hit me."

"Come on, Nick. You're not worried about anything. I couldn't possibly say anything that you wouldn't have an answer for. You say precisely what you mean to say. Nothing more, nothing less."

He sat back with a smile. "You think?"

"I know." She picked up her notebook, where she'd written several notes to herself so she could keep the interview on track. "Okay. Let's get started."

"Wait," Nick said, holding up his palm. "New rule."

Sara slumped with frustration. "What?"

"For every question you ask me, I get to ask you one."

"No. That wasn't part of our deal."

"It is now."

"That's not fair."

"Bad boys don't play fair. Don't you know that by now?"

Yes, she did. Which was why she should have anticipated that he wouldn't make this easy for her.

"It's not a big deal, Sara. It just lets me get to know you as well as you're getting ready to know me. What could be wrong with that?"

"Because this isn't about me."

He smiled. "For me it is."

Okay. She had a choice here. She knew if she didn't play his little game, he could very well walk right out the door. Or he could demand a different game that was even worse than this one. She let out a silent sigh, wishing she'd taken a few aspirin ahead of time for the headache she was sure she was going to get.

"Fine," she said. "A question for a question."

"Ladies first."

She looked at her notes. "Okay. I'd like a little background on you. Tell me about your education."

Nick took a sip of wine, then rested the glass on his knee. "Well, let's see. I graduated in the top ninety percent of my high school class, then went on to have a distinguished freshman year at Colorado State. I think I still hold the record for the number of tequila shots downed in one hour."

"And the next three years?"

"What next three years?"

Sara made a note: *Educational slacker.*

"My turn," Nick said. He set his wineglass down on the table, narrowed his eyes and stared deeply into hers. "What color panties are you wearing?"

Sara dropped her notebook to her lap. "What did you say?"

"Hey, you said I could ask questions. You didn't say what kinds of questions."

"You're not taking this seriously."

"On the contrary. I have a serious attraction to women's underwear."

And Sara had a serious desire to smack him one. Instead, she told herself not to overreact. She made a note: *Uses sexual innuendo to intimidate.* It was classic bad-boy behavior, and she knew the second she let him rattle her was the second she lost control of the situation.

"Blue," she said nonchalantly.

"Can I get some verification of that?"

"Is that one of your questions?"

"Yes."

"No. You can't. Now I get two questions in a row." She scanned her notes. "Why do you still date so many women when most men your age are ready to settle down?"

"For the same reason I like buffets rather than picking one item on the menu. See, I love women. All kinds of women. They're just so…" He sighed. "They look good, they smell good, they *taste* good…"

She made a note: *Sexually indiscriminate.* "Solid adult relationships should be about more than physical attraction."

"Maybe, but it sure starts things off with a bang, doesn't it?"

"Apparently you don't bother to dig much deeper than that. You love women like most men love their big-screen TVs. For the entertainment value."

"And that's why they love me, too. I'm not seeing the problem there."

"And that's the problem. Second question. What's the longest period of time you've ever dated one woman?"

"As in consecutive days?"

"Well, I was hoping for consecutive months or years, but I suppose you'll have to give me what you can."

"Let's put it this way. I'm a big fan of luxury hotels and long holiday weekends."

"Goodness, three whole days?" She made a note on her pad. "Gosh, Nick. For you that must be like a lifetime commitment."

"Hmm. I don't think sarcasm suits you, Sara."

"What makes you think I'm being sarcastic?"

"You know, for a serious researcher, you sure are biased."

"I never claimed to be unbiased. Why do you pursue such shallow relationships?"

"Nope. You already asked your two questions. Now it's my turn." He dropped his gaze to her breasts, then looked up again. "Matching bra?"

This man was hopeless.

"Yes, Nick," she said with exasperation. "My bra and panties are both blue. Silk with lace trim. Anything else you'd like to know about them?"

"No. That gives me a pretty good mental picture to play with."

She leaned away from him for a moment, giving him a studious look. "You know, I have to tell you. Speaking as a psychologist, your preoccupation with women's underwear is a little disconcerting."

He grinned. "Oh, yeah? Why is that?"

"Are you sure you're not a guy who…"

"Who what?"

She leaned closer and whispered, "Who likes women's underwear? You know. A little *too* much?"

His amused grin faded to a wary frown. "I like it on *women*. Not on *me*."

"You said you had a serious attraction to women's underwear."

"Not that kind of attraction!"

"It's nothing to be ashamed of. It's a fairly harmless fetish."

"Fetish?" He crinkled his face with disgust. "Listen, Sara—"

"Sometimes men don't actually wear it. They only like to touch it. Of course, sometimes that escalates to—"

"Hey! The only time I touch women's underwear is when it's on a *woman!*"

She drew back. "Well, you don't have to get so testy. I didn't bring up the subject. You did."

"Will you just ask the next question? And no more fetish talk."

"I believe we've already determined that the content of a question is up to the person asking it."

He twisted his mouth with irritation. "Fine. Ask."

Sara smiled furtively and referred to her notes again. She would have loved to ask him something about bathroom habits or penis size just to make her point further, but she did have a mission to accomplish here.

"A lot of the disconnection between men and women arises because of differing expectations for the future," she said. "What do you generally say to a woman at the end of a date?"

"Uh...thanks for the bacon and eggs?"

Sara stared at him with disbelief. "Do you sleep with every woman you go out with?"

"Oh, God, no."

"Well, that's good to hear."

"Sometimes we're just too darned busy to get a single wink of sleep."

She shook her head. This man was unbelievable. "How many women have you had sex with in the past year, anyway?"

"It's my turn to ask a question."

"No. I want to know. Five? ten? A hundred and ten?"

"Let's put it this way," he said. "As of tonight, it's one fewer than I'd like to."

She held her gaze steady. "I was looking for an absolute answer, not a relative one."

"Sorry. Right now I'm having a hard time thinking about all those other women."

"Give it up, Nick. I'm not buying your come-ons."

"What do you mean?"

"What's the real reason you pushed so hard to have dinner with me? We both know that genuine attraction isn't at the heart of it."

"We do?"

"I think it's a power play. I turned down your dinner invitation at the radio station, which you issued only because I was mad at you, and it was a blow to your ego. Men like you always rise to that challenge. But once you get what you want, you get bored and move on. What you don't realize is that a strong, intelligent woman won't buy into that kind of behavior."

"Sara, the key word in that sentence is *woman*. All those other adjectives are just space fillers."

"You wouldn't get to first base with a woman like that."

"You mean a woman like you?"

She stared at him evenly. "Yes."

"Sweetheart, forget first base. I'd hit the ball right out of the park." He leaned closer. "Then I'd take my own sweet time getting to home plate."

It was such a blatant attempt to get under her skin that Sara should have been able to brush it off instantly, but the power of that particular metaphor wasn't lost on her. Couple that with the fact that Nick had a talent for the kind of eye contact that made it almost impossible for her to look away, along with that deep, rich voice…

Get back on track.

"That's another characteristic of men like you," she said. "They talk a lot about scoring. About the end goal rather than the process."

"It's just the way men think. We're preprogrammed. We like to drive hard and get there fast, while women are more interested in taking in the sights along the way. You of all people should know that."

"Yes. I do. But it doesn't make your behavior any easier to tolerate."

"Okay," Nick said. "My turn." He eyed her carefully. "What's really bothering you, Sara?"

"What are you talking about?"

"Why do you write books about bad men? Did you get stood up at your high school prom, or what?"

"Actually, no. I graduated a year early to go to college, so I missed my high school prom."

"Ah. An overachiever. So what was your freshman year in college like?"

Sara shrugged. "Pretty average, I guess."

"Average would be partying too hard, drinking too much, then puking on your shoes the next day and wondering why you have a vague memory of dancing topless in the fountain outside the administration building."

"I take it back. I was decidedly above average."

"So how many years did it take you to get your undergrad degree?"

"Three."

"Let's see…that means you must have been twenty when you graduated."

"Nineteen. I started first grade when I was five."

"And when during that massive academic binge did you stop to have a good time?"

"This may come as a shock to you, but I enjoyed going to class."

"And I bet you enjoy working just as much."

"Yes, I do."

"Do you ever have any downtime? Say, over the holidays?"

"Of course. My mother is coming over on Christmas Eve for dinner, and then we're going to spend Christmas Day together. Just the two of us."

"No other relatives around?"

"I'm an only child. I have an aunt and uncle and a few cousins on the East Coast, but that's it. But my mother has moved back here now from St. Louis, so we finally have the opportunity to see each other more often."

"Well, thank God. I pictured you opening Christmas presents with one hand and poking at your PalmPilot with the other."

"I have plenty of leisure activities. They're just not the kinds of leisure activities you'd consider worthwhile."

"Like playing chess?"

"What?"

He nodded across the room at the small table that held her chessboard. "I don't believe I've ever known a woman who had one of those before."

"Forgive me, Nick, but I'm not too surprised by that."

He rose from the sofa.

"Where are you going?" she asked.

"Just having a closer look." He walked over to the chessboard and picked up one of the pieces. "Nice. What's it made of?"

"The pieces are pewter. The board is oak inlaid with mahogany."

"You must be a serious player."

"I used to be. I was on my collegiate chess team. We took second place in the national championship."

"Impressive."

"Do you play?" she asked.

"Well, I do know how the pieces are supposed to move."

Okay, so that had been a silly question. Asking Nick if he played chess was like asking an illiterate if he could quote Shakespeare.

He put the piece back down on the board. "Who do you play with these days?"

"I haven't played in a few years."

To her surprise, he grabbed their wineglasses, set them down on the table, pulled out a chair and sat down. "Then let's play now."

She blinked with surprise. "Now?"

"Yeah. Why not?"

"That's not what you're here for."

"Come on, Sara. It's early yet. Let's have a quick game. Then we can go back to work."

"No. I don't think so."

"Are you afraid of getting beaten?"

"Nick, your knowledge of the game appears to be limited to the movement of the pieces. That qualifies you to play chess like knowing how to drive a car qualifies you to race at Indy. Why would you want to be humiliated?"

"You can only be humiliated if your ego is tied up in winning. Is yours?"

"Of course not."

"Neither is mine. So let's play."

Okay. This didn't sound the least bit like Nick. Men like him didn't play chess. They played pool and darts, with an occasional game of Foosball thrown in. In her profession, atypical behavior was always a reason for a heads up, and her antennae were on the rise right now. He was definitely up to something, but she didn't know what.

Maybe it was time she found out.

"Fine." She sat down at the table. "Let's play."

"Good. This'll be fun."

"Not much fun, I'm afraid. It's going to be a short game." She nodded down at the board. "You're white, so you've got the first move."

"Oh, yeah. Okay."

He reached down, picked up one of his pawns, then stopped short. Slowly he turned his gaze up to meet hers. "What do you say we make this more interesting?"

Her antennae shot up a little further. "What do you mean?"

"Hmm…let's see." He sat back in his chair, twirling the pawn between his fingers. "How about we say that whoever loses a piece has to take something off?"

"What?"

"You know. Disrobe. Remove clothes. Undress."

Sara sat back, shaking her head incredulously. She knew he was up to something, but *strip chess?* Was there anything this man wouldn't do to digress into something sexual?

"Come on, Nick. Even you can't be serious about that."

"I never joke about getting naked."

"Are you out of your mind? I'm *not* playing strip chess with you!"

"Come on, Sara. It's my only hope."

"What are you talking about?"

"Unless I do something drastic, what other shot do I have at finding out if you're telling me the truth about your underwear?"

"There's that fetish again. You just can't keep your mind off it, can you?"

"I don't intend to wear women's underwear, but I'd sure like to see *you* wearing it."

"Give it up. I'm not playing strip *anything* with you."

Sudden realization flooded his face. "My God."

"What?"

"You really are afraid of getting beaten, aren't you?"

She drew back. "Beaten? Are you kidding me?"

"No. You are. You're a little rusty, and you're afraid you're going to lose."

"No."

"Yes. You're afraid a college dropout is going to humiliate you." He grinned. "And see you naked."

"I am not!"

He folded his arms over his chest. "Liar."

He was baiting her, plain and simple, which meant she should call a halt to this whole thing right now. Still, he'd touched that one nerve of hers that was permanently connected to the competitive side of her personality, the one that had been present ever since she wiped out the competition at the statewide spelling bee in the fourth grade. It just wasn't in her nature to back down from a challenge. And since the outcome here was hardly in question, would it really hurt to knock him down a peg or two? Of course, she'd move in for checkmate before he was totally naked, but toying with him right up to that point just might be the highlight of this whole evening.

"Okay, Nick. I'll play chess with you."

"Strip chess?"

"Yes. Strip chess." She rolled her eyes a little. "Well, those are two words I thought I'd never say in the same breath."

"Trust me, Sara," Nick said with a smile. "This is going to be fun."

Yes, she thought with a furtive smile. *It just might be.*

7

NICK MOVED A pawn forward one space, and Sara resisted the urge to snicker. Pawn to F3 was arguably the worst opening move a player could make. When she moved her king's knight to F6 and he countered with a pawn to H4, she started to wonder just how nice a body he had under those clothes and just how much of it she was going to make him reveal.

A few moves later, she captured one of those pawns with her knight.

Nick's mouth dropped open. "Now, why didn't I see that?"

"Don't feel bad," she said. "It was a beginner mistake. Now, which item of clothing would you like to remove?"

He tugged off a boot and tossed it aside, then turned his attention back to the board. He managed to sidestep her threat to his knight by moving it out of harm's way. Of course, that opened up another one of his pawns to attack, which she captured with her bishop.

"Shoot!" Nick said. "I didn't see that, either!"

"Another boot?"

He yanked it off and flung it next to the other one. A look of true determination came over his face, but still, after only four more moves for each of them, he was barefoot, too.

This was amazing. He was losing even faster than she'd anticipated. She gave him a big smile. "Are your feet cold?"

"My feet are just fine, thank you."

"Maybe I should turn the heat up now so it'll be warmer in here when you're stark naked."

"Can I get you some more wine?" Nick asked. "Say…a gallon or two?"

"Come on, Nick. You know I could drink half the wine product of northern California and still beat you." To make her point, she drained her wineglass and set it down on the table before making her next move.

"Just think," she said as she scooted her pawn into position, "pretty soon I won't have to ask you that age-old question. I'll know firsthand."

"What's that?"

"Boxers…or briefs?"

He glared at her. "Well, aren't you the funny one?"

"Come on, Nick. Where's your sense of humor?"

"Don't get cocky. This game's not over yet."

"I've got news for you," she said. "This game was over before it even got started."

"Be quiet. I'm thinking." He looked over the board, his brow furrowed with concentration. "Let's see. If I go here, you'll get me there. If I go here, you'll…no, wait. I can't do that. Bishops move diagonally, not up and down."

Good Lord. This was like shooting fish in a barrel.

"Oh, what the hell," he said, finally moving a pawn right into the gaping jaws of her rook. A more sympathetic person would at least have acted as if she were considering what move to make next, but any man who inquired about the color of a woman's panties was getting no sympathy from her. She immediately bumped the pawn with her rook and removed it from the board.

"Damn it!" Nick said. "Why didn't I see that?"

"Got me." She glanced down at his feet. "And look at that. You're all out of shoes and socks."

"Okay, now," he said a little nervously. "This strip chess thing. Maybe we need to rethink that."

"Oh, no. No way. You set the rules, and we're playing by them. But take heart. I suspect I'll have checkmate before I see anything of yours you wouldn't show me on a beach."

She felt a rush of power. *Ha.* It was time for him to be objectified. See how he liked it. And she intended to leer at him just as much as she possibly could.

"I believe your sweater is next?" she said. "Unless you'd prefer taking off your jeans."

With a tight-lipped glare, he leaned away from the table. He pulled his sweater off over his head, and she got a shock.

No shirt? No T-shirt, even? It was ten below. What man didn't wear something under his sweater?

As he tossed his sweater over the back of her sofa, suddenly she was looking at his bare chest, and God, what a sight it was. Broad and muscled but not to excess, sprinkled with just enough hair to define his form without masking any of it. Couple that with strong shoulders and biceps, and he was pretty much perfection. She knew her mouth was probably hanging open, but she couldn't seem to shut it.

No. She had to stop staring at him as if she were in awe, no matter how true it was. She managed to morph her expression into a more subtle one, letting her gaze wander deliberately over his naked chest as if she surveyed men's bodies all the time.

"Very nice, Nick," she said, "You must work out."

He scowled at her, but still she continued to look at him.

Finally he crossed his arms over his chest. "Will you stop staring at me so we can get on with this?"

She gave him a lazy smile. "Sure, Nick. Whatever you say."

As he leaned in to consider his next move, Sara sat back and watched with amusement as he poured every bit of his concentration into the game. Suddenly she realized how good she felt. The wine was making her head swim in a most delightful manner, she was putting a very arrogant man in his place and the view from where she was sitting had just gotten a whole lot better.

She giggled to herself. Life was *good*.

Then Nick captured her bishop.

Sara sat up suddenly and stared at the board. "Wait a minute. What did you just do?"

"I moved my knight and took your bishop. I did it right, didn't I?"

"Show me again what you did."

He did an instant replay, which she examined from all angles. "Yes. Okay. You did it right. Good for you, Nick."

He grinned. "What's the matter? Didn't see me coming?"

"Even the best players can't anticipate every move."

"Okay, Sara. Off with it."

With an offhand shrug, she pulled off one of her shoes, which was really no big deal. Even as inept as he was, sooner or later he was bound to take at least one of her pieces.

She turned back to the board and made a move, then sat back. Nick surveyed the situation, his chin in his hand, tapping his finger against his cheek. Then he raised his eyebrows, picked up his rook and took one of her pawns.

Sara blinked with surprise.

"I can do that, can't I?" he asked.

Her heart began to beat faster. "Uh…yeah. You can do that."

Okay. He'd just made a few lucky moves. And she still had plenty of clothes to take off before she got down to anything critical. She slipped off her other shoe and nudged it aside. There was no need to worry yet.

Half a dozen moves later, though, when she'd lost both of her socks, she decided that maybe worry was warranted after all.

What the hell was happening here?

She didn't get this. Nick's play seemed almost haphazard, yet he was gaining a foothold. Of course, she hadn't been playing carefully before, thinking she could easily beat him, so now her board position was weak, with her pawn clusters doing her no good at all and her king still not castled. Why hadn't she been playing smarter?

Well, he wasn't taking anything else. No *way* was he taking anything else.

Unfortunately, the wine that had made her feel so wonderful before was now muddling her mind, making it hard for her to think straight. Her heart was beating like crazy, and the pieces seemed to swim together until she could barely tell one from another.

Then she saw it. Yes! A way to move in on his king that she knew he couldn't possibly anticipate. And two moves subsequent to that, she'd have checkmate. She shifted her knight from E4 to F6. Ha! Let him deal with *that*.

His gaze narrowed. "Are you sure you want to do that?"

She froze. Uh…yeah. Of course she did. At least she thought she did. Didn't she?

Wait a minute. Hell, yes, she did. He was just trying to rattle her into thinking it was a bad move so she'd change it. And who was he to question her moves, anyway?

"Yes, Nick. That's my move. Now it's your move."

He shrugged offhandedly, picked up his knight and captured one of her pawns.

She felt a shot of panic. "Now, wait a minute! What did you just do?"

"Are you going to ask me that every time I move?"

"Yes!"

"Actually, I think it was quite clear. I moved my knight from C2 to D4 and captured your pawn. That gives me better control of the center of the board at the same time it opens a file for my rook. Of course, it also means I've got two of your pieces in a knight fork."

Her gaze snapped up to meet his. "*What* did you say?"

A wicked smile crept across his face, and suddenly she felt sick. It couldn't be. It just *couldn't*. There was no way…

"You tricked me!"

"And you bought it. You assumed I didn't know how to play the game."

"You told me you didn't!"

"Not exactly. I told you I knew how the pieces moved. Your expectation filled in the rest."

Sara's mouth hung open in disbelief. "Where the *hell* did you learn how to play chess?"

"From my father. He's a college professor. So is my mother. It's what intellectuals do, isn't it?"

Sara was aghast. "Your parents are college professors?"

"Yeah. A real shocker, huh?"

"You lied to me!"

"Nope. I never lied. You just jumped to the conclusion that I was an idiot."

"But—"

"Hey, you're the chess champ. I'm just a dumb schmuck

who picked up the game from his old man. Shouldn't you still be able to beat me?"

"Doesn't matter," she said. "This game is over."

"That's funny," he said. "You didn't want to stop before, but now that I'm winning—"

"You aren't winning!"

"Sweetheart, I know you've got all those letters after your name, but trust me. When it comes to chess, you don't stand a chance against me."

Sara swallowed hard, her face growing hot. She felt like a complete fool. She should have known. She should have known never to let her guard down around this man. *Never.*

He picked up her knight. "And what item of clothing do I get to trade this for?"

Then it struck her. Her shirt came next.

"I'm not taking off anything else!"

Nick shook his head slowly, then rose to his feet. He eased around the table wearing nothing but a pair of jeans and a look on his face that said he had things in mind she couldn't possibly envision. Her heart was thumping so hard she thought it was going to burst right through her chest.

"Nick? What are you doing?"

He came up behind her chair. She started to turn around, but he put his hands against her shoulders and leaned down, his hot breath fanning her ear. "I believe we had a deal."

He slid his hands from her shoulders to the front of her neck, then moved them slowly across her collarbone until his fingers found the top button of her shirt.

He flicked it open.

Sara swallowed a gasp. His fingers descended to the next button. The moment he flicked it open, too, she grabbed his hands to still them.

"Now, Sara," Nick whispered against her ear. "I thought you were a woman of your word."

"This is just a game," she said, breathing hard, fighting a flush of sexual awareness so intense it was almost painful. "And it's time to stop now."

She pushed his hands away and stood up, pulling the sides of her shirt together. She sidestepped her chair to walk away, only to feel Nick's hands on her shoulders again, easing her to a halt.

"Hold on, Sara. We're not finished yet."

His grip was so gentle that she could have easily slipped away, but some force she couldn't fathom kept her from doing it. He moved his hands from her shoulders to her elbows and back up again in long, soothing strokes, easing up behind her at the same time, so close she could feel the heat of his body mingling with hers.

"I'll make you a deal," Nick said. "You can keep your shirt on. But you'll have to give me something in return."

Before she could ask him what that might be, he lifted one hand from her shoulder, and she was surprised to feel his fingertips slowly pull a pin from her hair. That simple, almost imperceptible touch made her stomach swoop with exhilaration.

The pin plinked to the tabletop. He took out another one. Then another. Slowly, slowly he pulled out a fourth pin, and her hair fell in a loose cascade over her shoulders.

"There," he whispered. "That's better. Your hair is way too pretty to wear up."

"Nick—"

"Shh."

He moved his hand around her waist, splaying his fingers against her abdomen and easing forward until the length of his body was pressed against hers. With a slow sweep of his hand, he pushed her hair behind her shoulder, the tips of his fingers brushing her bare skin, then leaned in and kissed the side of her neck. A thousand nerve endings leaped to life. Ten thousand. *Millions.*

This couldn't be happening. She couldn't be standing here at the mercy of Nick's hands and his lips and his whispered words tickling her ear, as if she had no control over anything anymore. But that was exactly what she was doing, falling so hard and so fast into the spell he was weaving she couldn't even form the word *no* in her mind, much less say it.

He trailed kisses along her neck, and her knees went weak. It was such a cliché, but all at once her legs felt as if they literally weren't going to hold her up. The rest of her muscles followed suit, becoming limp and useless. She slid her hand over his where it rested against her abdomen, her fingers flexing involuntarily against his.

"I have a feeling," he whispered, "that you have one erogenous zone no man has ever found."

Just the term *erogenous zone* was enough to make her sweat, because she couldn't remember a man she'd been with who'd spent much time hunting for any of hers.

"What's that?" she asked.

"Your brain. And you hate that. You hate like hell dating men who have no clue how to get inside that mind of yours. Who can barely connect to you physically, much less mentally. But me…" He pressed his lips to her neck again, sending shivers coursing through her whole body. "I found your mind the moment we met, and I've been touching it ever since."

It was true. When she was with Nick, her mind felt fully engaged, hovering in that frustrating but invigorating place where she was never quite sure what was going to happen next. In the regimented, predictable world she'd built for herself, every move he made and every word he spoke seemed to shoot adrenaline straight to her heart.

But she knew that wasn't the real world. Nick was an anomaly. A diversion. So unlike the kind of man she pictured herself with that she couldn't even fathom that this was happening.

"Nick," she whispered. "I can't do this."

"Why not?"

"Because you're not the kind of man—"

"Not the kind of man you should want? God, Sara, you're dying for a man like me."

"No."

"Yes. You're dying for a man who makes you feel alive. Who turns every molecule of his attention to you and makes you feel as if you're the only woman on earth."

"Nick—"

"A man who's exciting and unpredictable, who frustrates you and irritates you, but only because he's making you think and feel things you've never thought or felt before and you just don't know how to deal with it. A man who can't wait to drive you absolutely wild in ways you can't even imagine."

He turned her around and pulled her right up next to him. She put her hands against his shoulders in a weak attempt to put distance between them, but the moment she touched him, her urge to push him away vanished. Instead, she just stared into those incredible blue eyes, unable to move, unable to think.

Unable to resist.

He bent his head, his lips hovering over hers. "You want all those things as much as you want your next breath. And that's exactly what I'm going to give you."

He slipped his fingers through her hair at the nape of her neck, pulled her forward and smothered her mouth with a kiss. Sara's whole body jolted with surprise, but he held her tightly, slipping his tongue between her parted lips and sweeping it against hers. His kiss was raw and hot and possessive, with a carnal edge that shocked her. And unbelievably, she was letting him do it. She was standing in her living room in Nick Chandler's arms, letting him kiss her in a way that made her mind go blank and her insides turn to mush. And then she wasn't just letting him kiss her.

She was kissing him back.

She slid one hand around his neck, pulling him even harder against her, tilting her head until their mouths were joined in the most intimate way possible. Breathless already, her head began to reel, but it only intensified the adrenaline rush and made her want more. She pressed her other hand to his chest, loving the feel of the hard muscle there and the sensation of his heart pounding beneath her palm.

So this is what it's supposed to feel like.

That thought filled her mind, colliding with a montage of other men's kisses she'd experienced over the years, those bland, boring, halfhearted attempts that had been cool and hesitant and had left her dying for more. Dying for *this*. And now she wondered what other wondrous things might be out there that she'd been missing all her life.

She had a feeling this man knew every one of them.

His fingers moved to her shirt buttons again, opening another one, then another, until cool air hit her chest. Still kissing her, he slipped his hand inside her shirt, his fingertips locating the front clasp of her bra with laser beam precision.

As he flicked it open, though, a glimmer of discomfort rose inside her, and her mind started to swim back to reality. As Nick pushed the cups away from her breasts and pressed his hand to her naked flesh, all at once it dawned on her what she was doing.

And who she was doing it with.

She pulled away suddenly, twisting away from him and yanking the sides of her shirt together. "What are you *doing*?"

He stared at her, breathing hard, his eyes wide. "What do you mean, what am I doing?"

She couldn't believe it. She'd almost…she'd come so close to…with *Nick Chandler?*

"Sara?"

She turned away, scrambling to hook her bra. He took a step toward her.

"No!" she said. "Stay away from me!"

She buttoned her blouse, humiliation rising inside her.

"What's the matter?" he asked.

"I can't believe I fell for this!"

Nick looked at her incredulously. "Fell for what?"

She waved her hand around her apartment. "This!"

"What are you talking about?"

"Dinner. Wine. Dim lights. All the sexual talk. And strip chess? For God's sake. What kind of ploy was that?"

He shook his head with confusion. "Now, wait a minute. I thought we were past that. *Way* past."

"This is what men like you do. You coerce. You intimidate. You do anything you can to get a woman into bed!"

Frustration ran wild on his face. "Well, what was I supposed to do? Play by your rules? That would have gotten me exactly nowhere. That wall you throw up is a pretty formidable one, Sara. I didn't expect it to come tumbling down all by itself."

"Does it have to tumble down all in one night?"

"I just wanted to shake you up a little. Make you admit that there's an attraction here—"

"There isn't!"

"Oh, *please.* I've never engaged in so much vertical fore-play with a woman in my life!"

"Exactly! That's *exactly* how men like you behave! You can't even have a simple conversation with a woman without turning it into something sexual! And we could have gone to a different restaurant, but no. You came here because you wanted to get me into bed."

"I came here," he said sharply, "because I wanted to be alone with you. To get to know you. To see where things might lead."

"If you have your way, straight to the bedroom."

"I know what you think of me, Sara. But did it ever occur to you that you might be wrong about my motives?"

"Not for one moment. I know exactly who you are, Nick. After all, you profess it for an hour every day on the radio."

She gave him a challenging stare, and he returned it with one of his own, his blue eyes suddenly charged with anger.

"And I know who you are, too," he said. "You're a woman who has made a career out of teaching other women how to resist men like me. Well, let me tell you something, sweetheart. You're sure having a hell of a hard time practicing what you preach."

Sara swallowed hard, tears burning behind her eyes. She opened her mouth to speak, but she couldn't. She couldn't say a single word.

Because he was right.

Suddenly the magnitude of what she'd done hit her full force. She couldn't look at him anymore. She had to get out of there *now.*

She spun around, went down the hall into her bedroom and closed the door. She caught sight of herself in the mirror, her mussed hair, her flushed cheeks, and her shirt buttoned wrong.

Oh, God. What had she done?

A minute later, she heard her front door open and close, and she knew he'd left her apartment. Then…silence.

She sat down on the bed, tears filling her eyes, angry at Nick, but even more angry at herself. She'd underestimated him so completely that she ought to have her license revoked. She should have known that any man with his verbal ability had a few brain cells to back it up. But given what he did for a living, how could she have known just how smart he really was?

Smart enough to manipulate her right to the point of going to bed with him.

She fell back on her bed and stared at the ceiling. What in the hell had she done? If anyone found out—

She sat bolt upright again, her heart beating madly with apprehension. All at once it dawned on her what had really happened here tonight. Getting her into bed hadn't been Nick's only goal.

He wanted to get her into bed so he could tell his listeners all about it.

The sudden realization of what she'd done made her stomach swim with shame and disgrace. Tomorrow afternoon, she was going to turn on the radio and hear Nick broadcast her humiliation to the entire city of Boulder. He would tell his listeners how he'd brought dinner to her house, conned her into playing strip chess, kissed her until she lost all sense of reality and then had her very nearly naked in her living room.

And the moment those words came out of his mouth, every bit of the professional credibility she'd worked so hard to build over the years would be destroyed.

8

THE NEXT DAY, Sara asked Karen to come to her office so she could break the news about what had happened between her and Nick, not to mention that she was going to need a shoulder to cry on as she listened to the radio broadcast from hell.

Karen showed up a few minutes before Nick's show and, as Sara told her what had happened, Karen's eyes got progressively wider, reaching maximum dilation when she mentioned a certain game they'd played.

"Strip chess?" Karen said. "Are you telling me you played *strip chess* with Nick Chandler?"

"Please stop saying it out loud. *Please.*"

"God, Sara, what were you thinking?"

"I don't know! We ate dinner, we had a few glasses of wine, and then I started interviewing him, and somehow we got around to playing chess, and then he suggested… you know…"

"And you agreed to that?"

"I was sure I could beat him!"

"Wait a minute. Nick Chandler beat *you* at chess?"

"Not completely. It didn't get that far."

"Just how naked did you get?"

Sara described what had happened next, and that horrified expression came over Karen's face again. "Sara, please tell me you're joking. Please tell me you weren't standing half-naked in your living room kissing Nick Chandler."

"Hey! You were the one who told me I should get up close and personal with him!"

"I was teasing you, Sara! I didn't think you'd actually do it! I thought you were smart enough not to—" She stopped short and let out a breath. "I'm sorry. I didn't mean that. I—wait. He's coming on."

Karen hurried over to the stereo and turned it up, then sat down on the sofa with Sara. They listened to Nick do his usual monologue at the top of his show, telling his listeners what was on tap for that day. Then he did a phone interview with a woman who claimed to have had sex with an alien before he finally got around to taking phone calls. Not surprisingly, the first caller asked about Sara.

"I've got David from Broomfield on the line," Nick said. "Seems he wants to ask me about my evening with Sara Davenport."

Sara put her hand against her stomach, sure she was going to be sick.

"Hey, Nick!" David said. "How come you didn't show up at Luigi's last night?"

"Now, David. How do you know I didn't show up at Luigi's?"

"Because I was there!"

"Well, there you go. Don't you think I know you guys are smart enough to head to my favorite restaurant to watch the action? Sara and I went somewhere else. After all, when I'm out to seduce a woman, two's company and twenty's a crowd."

So he was admitting it. That was what he'd been up to all along. Sara closed her eyes, feeling like a complete fool.

"So where'd you go?" David asked.

"Come on, man. If I told you all my secrets, I'd never have any privacy at all, would I?"

Sara blinked with surprise. "He's not going to tell them he came to my apartment?"

"Shh!" Karen said.

"So she was going to interview you, right?" David said. "What kind of stuff did she ask you?"

"Not much, really. A lot of boring psychological stuff I wasn't really following, kinda like when they show you those pieces of paper with blotches on them and ask you what you see, and then they nod their heads and go, 'Hmm,' and you never really know if you said the right thing or not."

Sara couldn't believe this. Boring psychological stuff? What was he talking about?

"Sounds as if it was a real bore all the way around," David said.

"Oh, no. Not completely. Not when the view was that spectacular."

"So she really is a ten after all?"

"I had to use my imagination a little since she was still pretty buttoned-up, but yeah. Definitely a ten."

Buttoned-up? She'd been unbuttoned, unpinned *and* unhooked, not to mention on the verge of sexual explosion, and he wasn't saying a word about it?

"So..." David said, dragging his voice out suggestively. "What happened between you two?"

Nick paused for a few seconds, during which time Sara saw her life flash before her eyes. *Oh, God. Here it comes.*

"Just between you and me, David, she wouldn't even let me close enough to lay a hand on her."

Sara sat back with disbelief. Not close enough to lay a

hand on her? She still felt hot at the very thought of how he'd laid his hands all *over* her.

"Are you telling me you struck out?" David said.

"Hey, it wasn't for lack of trying! I hit on that lady every which way I could think of, but I'm afraid she really does practice what she preaches."

The echo of Nick's words from last night boomed inside Sara's head, only now he'd turned them around and was making her sound like a paragon of virtue. Why wasn't he telling them what really happened?

"I offered to take her for a little walk on the wild side," Nick went on, "but unfortunately Sara Davenport is still the poster girl for good behavior." He sighed dramatically. "I'm just hoping I'll get lucky one day and she'll change her mind. Sara? If you're out there, you know where to find me."

Sara looked at Karen, their stunned expressions mirror images of each other's.

"I'm going to take a little break now," Nick said, "but when I come back, I have something special for the ladies. This man claims to have the world's largest..." He paused. "Tell you what. During the break, why don't you try to figure out what he has that's bigger than the average man's? I'll be right back."

As a commercial for a local car dealer came on, Sara sat back on the sofa, dumbstruck. "My God. He didn't tell them."

"Yeah," Karen said. "Imagine that."

"What he said is actually *good* for my reputation. He could have trashed me. And he didn't."

"Suppose he has something bigger in mind?"

"What?"

"Maybe he wants to lure you in, then get you to actually sleep with him before he goes public with it."

Sara considered that, but somehow she didn't think so. "I don't know. I guess it's possible."

"Well, be careful. Stay as far away from him as you can and it'll never be an issue."

Weak with relief, Sara flicked off the radio. "You know, Karen, maybe I underestimated him."

"What do you mean?"

She shrugged. "I don't know. Thinking back now…well, Nick was actually a little different than I thought he was going to be."

"How so?"

"I don't know. It was only at the end of the evening that things got kind of ugly. Before that, of course he was coming on to me, but still I was actually kind of…"

"Kind of what?"

"Kind of…having a good time."

Karen stared at her a moment, and then her eyes got big and horrified. "No, Sara. Don't even think it."

"What?"

"You want to see him again, don't you?"

Sara turned away. "Of course not."

"Look me in the eye and say that."

Sara slowly turned back. She opened her mouth to deny it, only to close it again with a sigh.

"Oh, my God! Sara, don't you dare go there. I know I teased you before about having hot sweaty sex with him, but that was only because I thought you'd never even consider it. You do *not* want to have anything to do with him!"

"Don't worry, Karen. It's not smart to see him again, and I'm not going to."

"If you do and people find out, your credibility will be shot. I'm a hell of a good publicist, but even I can't fix that."

"I know."

"He found a shred of conscience this time. Don't count on it happening again."

"Come on, Karen. Give me some credit, will you? I dodged this bullet. I have no intention of putting myself back into the line of fire."

"No matter how sexy he is?"

Sara sighed with resignation. "Yes. No matter how sexy he is."

"Good." Karen was silent for a moment, as if mulling something over. She raised an eyebrow. "So tell me. Was he a good kisser?"

Sara closed her eyes as the memory filled her mind. "You have no idea."

"Strip chess. I gotta say that's pretty creative. The most inventive thing a man's ever done to get me into bed was drop his pants and say, 'Hey, baby, wanna do it?'" She huffed with disgust. "Imagine how my toes tingled when I heard that."

Sara's toes were tingling right now just thinking about how Nick had kissed her last night. She hadn't known what it felt like to have her mind fully engaged in the moment and buzzing with excitement, her nerves on alert, her heart beating with exhilaration. Now she knew what women were facing when it came to resisting that kind of man. She knew firsthand how it felt to be on that emotional roller coaster, and just how tempting it was for a woman to return to a man like Nick again and again, no matter how bad he was for her.

If you change your mind, you know where to find me…

No. She'd told Karen the truth. She intended to have nothing more to do with Nick Chandler. But still, there was one thing that didn't make sense.

If Nick was the bad boy she thought he was, he would have told everyone within the sound of his voice every detail of what had happened between them, exploiting their encounter for his own personal gain. But he hadn't.

The question was…why hadn't he?

SEVERAL DAYS LATER, Nick was driving through falling snow and evening traffic to his producer's house. It was time once again for that party of parties: Butch's annual Christmas Eve blowout, which had little to do with the holiday and a lot to do with eating, drinking and being merry.

Nick glanced at Ted. "You know how stupid those antlers look, don't you?"

Ted pulled down the passenger visor mirror and turned his head left and right, examining his foam reindeer antlers. "Stupid? You think? I was going for festive."

"I'm surprised you didn't wear ones that light up."

"Damn! I didn't think of that. Is the mall still open?"

Nick rolled his eyes.

Ted smacked the visor back up. "Hey, from the way you describe this party of Butch's, I'll fit right in with the crowd."

Ted was right. He'd fit in with no problem. This year, for some reason, Nick was the one who felt out of place.

In the past, he'd looked forward to Butch's party, where everyone drank to excess, played stupid Christmas parody songs and in general went a little wild. Nick always let the girls sit on his lap and tell him what they wanted for Christmas, and a few times, before the night was over, he'd given at least one of them her wish.

But this year he just wasn't up for it.

He pulled up to a stoplight and turned to Ted. "Why do I hang around for this party every year? Why don't I just go to Colorado Springs on Christmas Eve instead of waiting until Christmas morning?"

"Uh…because the women are more fun here than your family is there?"

"Oh, yeah? What kind of woman goes to a party at Butch's house on Christmas Eve, anyway?"

"The kind with no family in town, who's too broke to fly home, who wants to get drunk and get laid and isn't picky about what day it happens to be."

Nick sighed. "Oh, yeah. That kind of woman."

"Come on, man. You go every year, don't you? What's so different about this one?"

Nick wasn't sure. All he knew was that he just didn't want to be there tonight.

"You know," Ted said, "you've been in a really crappy mood for the past few days."

"No, I haven't."

"Trust me. You have. You want to tell me why?"

"There's nothing to tell."

"Yeah. Right."

Nick shot him an angry look. "I said I haven't been in a crappy mood."

"Okay. Okay. I hear you." Ted looked away, rolling his eyes. "Gee, I wonder where I ever got *that* idea?"

The light turned green and Nick hit the gas. Hell, yes, he'd been in a crappy mood. And for good reason. But the last thing he wanted to do was talk about why.

Several minutes later, he pulled up in front of Butch's house. The music was already so loud that Nick could hear it faintly even sitting inside his car. It was clearly one of those nights where the cops would be coming to the door to tell Butch to knock off the noise.

"Uh-oh," Ted said, glancing past Nick. "Look who's here."

Nick turned to see a tall blond woman approaching his car. Yep. The night was already complete, and he hadn't even stepped out of the car.

"Why the hell did Butch invite her?" Ted asked.

"He didn't. Raycine is never invited. She's a professional party crasher."

She leaned over and knocked on the driver's window. Nick lowered it with a sigh of resignation. He could deal with Raycine now, or he could deal with her later. Might as well get it out of the way.

She flicked her phony blond hair over her shoulder, then folded her arms on the car door and gave Nick a big smile. She reminded him of a cat getting ready to gobble up a canary.

"Hey, Nick."

"Raycine."

"Heard your show a few days ago, and I'm thinking you've got some dirt for me. What's with you and the up-tight psychologist?"

Nick's heart skipped. "Nothing. She just interviewed me for a book she's writing. That's all."

"Come on, Nick," Raycine said. "Your listeners may have bought all that nonsense about you striking out, but I'm not one of those eighteen- to thirty-four-year-old party animals who tunes in to your show because I love hearing men behaving badly. I'm listening for other things. Know what I mean?"

"I'm afraid there's nothing else to tell."

"Now, you know I don't know the meaning of the words, *No comment*. If you don't give me something, you know I'll have to extrapolate."

Nick knew exactly what she was talking about. She'd extrapolated several times where his love life was concerned, pairing him with everyone from a supermodel on a ski trip to a porn star to a set of twenty-year-old triplets. Okay, so the supermodel story was true, but she'd really gone out on a limb for the others. Those times hadn't been that big a deal, though, because the women concerned hadn't minded being linked to him whether the story was true or not.

He didn't think Sara would be quite as enthusiastic.

"I have a feeling something else is going on," Raycine said.

"If something else were going on, wouldn't I have talked about it on my show?"

"Maybe." She paused. "And maybe not. I'm watching you, Nick. *Both* of you." Raycine backed away from his car. She gave him a sly wink, then turned and walked toward the house.

Ted made a sound of disgust. "I thought reptiles were supposed to be dormant in the winter."

"I don't want her bothering Sara. I swear to God, if she does, I'll—"

He stopped short and looked away.

"If she does, you'll what?"

Nick was silent.

Ted stared at him with disbelief. "My God. Raycine's right. Something's going on between you two."

"No, it isn't."

"Oh, yes it is. Something's been eating you, and it has to do with Sara Davenport. What is it?"

"You heard my show. You know everything that happened."

"So you struck out, huh?"

"Yep."

"Kinda surprising. Are you losing your touch?"

"No, I'm not losing my touch. We just never hooked up. That's all."

Ted shook his head sadly. "Nick, you're going to tell me what's wrong sooner or later. So why don't we save a little time and make it sooner?"

Nick shot him a look of supreme irritation. If Ted ever got stuck on something, getting him unstuck was pretty much impossible. Nick hated that.

He also hated it when Ted was right.

"If I tell you what happened," Nick said, "it's going no further than this car, do you hear me?"

"Kid, if I was inclined to tell people everything I know about you, you'd probably be in jail today."

Nick gave Ted the *Reader's Digest* version of what had happened between him and Sara. And by the time he finished, the man was grinning like crazy.

"You gotta be kidding me. You got her to play strip chess?"

"Yeah, and it was a really crappy thing for me to do."

"Sounds pretty inspired to me."

"No, it wasn't. I never stopped for five seconds to consider who I was dealing with."

"What do you mean?"

"Sara isn't some bimbo I can crook my finger at and she'll follow me into the bedroom."

"I don't know. Sounds to me like that was exactly where she was heading."

"Are you not getting this? She writes books teaching women how to resist men like me, and I coerced her into getting half-naked in her living room. And now she hates me."

"Hey, you didn't twist her arm."

"Oh, yes I did. And I made her feel like a fool in the process. But I don't care how her reputation says she's supposed to behave. She did nothing wrong." Nick frowned. "She just did it with the wrong man."

Ted shook his head. "I never thought I'd see the day."

"What?"

"When you'd fall for a woman. Especially a woman like Sara Davenport."

"That's not what's happening here."

"Then what is happening?"

"I just feel bad about the way I treated her. That's all."

"So apologize to her."

Nick sighed. "She'd probably just slam the door in my face."

"Then there's nothing you can do. Come on, kid. It's time to drown your sorrows. Let's party."

With a sigh of resignation, Nick pulled his gloves out of his pockets. When he did, something came out with them and clicked to the console, then fell on the floor near his feet. He leaned over and picked it up. A plastic knob?

Then he remembered. It was the dimmer switch knob from Sara's dining room. He'd stuck it in his coat pocket to keep her from finding it.

He remembered back to that night, to the moment he finally had Sara in his arms and was kissing her. Everything had been great right up to the point when she realized who she was standing half-naked with in her living room. Nick had picked up the phone about a dozen times since then, thinking he ought to apologize, but he always talked himself out of it. After all, she probably never wanted to speak to him again, so what would be the point? And after what had happened between them, she certainly wouldn't think of interviewing him again.

But now, if he had to return this to her…

Okay. So it was a lousy excuse to see her. But if it could get him in the door, it was worth a try.

"There's something I have to do," Nick said. "I'll be back in a little while."

"Hey, you can't just leave me here. You drove."

"I said I'd be back later."

"Does this have anything to do with Sara?"

Nick turned the knob over in his fingers. "Yeah. It does."

"Okay. Fine. But you'd better get your ass back here pretty soon or the girls are going to stage a riot."

"Just go in there and sweep them off their feet. They'll forget all about me."

"Right. I'm just the substitute for Nick Chandler they've been looking for." Ted got out of the car, his reindeer antlers flopping against the door frame, then stuck his head back in. "Now, don't get sidetracked and forget where you left me."

"I won't."

As Ted slammed the door and made his way up the sidewalk, Nick reached down to start the car.

No. Wait a minute. He couldn't just show up unannounced at Sara's house. After all, it was Christmas Eve, and her mother was coming for dinner. She wouldn't want him intruding on that.

Then again, maybe that would be a good thing. If he charmed her mother a little, maybe she'd have a little influence over her daughter.

Oh, hell, who was he kidding? If Sara saw him standing on her front porch, she probably wouldn't even open the door.

Finally he decided that the best thing to do was to call first to try to break the ice. He phoned directory assistance, got her number and dialed it. As the phone rang twice, three times, his mouth went dry and his heart hammered in his chest.

Finally the line clicked.

"Hello?"

"Sara. It's Nick."

There was a moment of silence, then, "Nick? What do you want?"

She didn't sound the least bit happy to hear from him. Then again, had he expected her to be? Suddenly he felt like a total idiot.

"I...well, it was the funniest thing. You know the other night when I was at your apartment, and I took the knob off the dimmer switch? Well, I stuck it in my coat pocket. I just now found it. Now, I know you weren't too thrilled about me dimming the lights and all that, but the fact remains...well, you know...I've got this knob, and I know you must want it back. I was going to be out tonight, so I thought if I could drop by for just a minute..."

Dead silence on the line. Five seconds passed. Then ten. Oh, hell. What had made him think this was a good idea?

"Sara?"

"Never mind about the knob," she said. "I don't care if I get it back."

He heard a catch in her voice, a slight slurring of her words, and for a moment he was confused. Then it dawned on him.

She was crying.

"Sara? What's wrong?"

"Nothing's wrong."

"Is your mother there?"

Another stretch of silence. "No. She's not."

"It's getting late. Why isn't she there?"

"That's none of your business."

"Is everything all right?"

He heard her sniff. "Yes. Everything's fine."

"Are you by yourself?"

"Yes."

"Sara? Tell me what's wrong."

"I have to go."

He heard a click. He pulled the phone away from his ear and stared at it a moment, wondering what to do.

No. He knew what to do. It was Christmas Eve, Sara was alone and she was crying.

He tossed down his cell phone, started his car and headed to her apartment.

9

WHAT ARE YOU crying for? As if something like this has never happened before?

Sara jerked one more tissue out of the box beside her on the sofa and dabbed at her eyes, but the tears still came, blurring the Christmas tree and the candles and the glow from the fireplace into a big, hazy mess.

In a surge of anger, she got up from the sofa, blew out all the candles, shut off the gas log in the fireplace and the lights on the Christmas tree. After all, what was the point of keeping any of those things lit? It only burned down a bunch of expensive candles and raised her utility bill for nothing.

Absolutely nothing.

She kicked off her shoes and flopped back down onto the sofa, feeling angry and frustrated and heartbroken all at the same time, wondering if there would ever come a day when she'd quit getting her hopes up about things that were never going to happen.

She wished she could call Karen, but her friend had left town this morning for her brother's house in Grand Junction and wouldn't be back until New Year's Day. The last thing Sara wanted to do was call her there and ruin her Christmas Eve, too.

Then she heard a knock at her door.

She rose and looked out the peephole, and her heart leaped right into her throat. Nick?

She turned around quietly and pressed her back to the door. What was he doing here? Had he actually come here to return something to her that she didn't care about in the first place? And on Christmas Eve?

He knocked again. She closed her eyes. *Please go away. Just please, please go away.*

"Come on, Sara! I know you're in there!"

He knocked some more. *Damn.* The last thing she needed was for somebody to see Nick Chandler banging on her apartment door.

She opened the door. "Will you cut that out? Somebody's going to hear you!"

He pushed the door open and came inside, shutting it behind him.

"You shouldn't be here," she said.

"Tell me what's wrong."

"Nothing's wrong. Just go. Please, just—"

"No. Something's wrong. And I'm not leaving until you tell me what it is."

She put her hand to her forehead for a moment, her head pounding. The last thing she wanted to do was stand here and spill all the details of her dysfunctional family Christmas, and to Nick Chandler, of all people.

"I heard you crying on the phone," he said softly. "Please tell me what's wrong."

She told herself she couldn't trust him. Not after what he'd done the other night. Then she thought about how he could have revealed all that to his listeners and ruined her career, yet he'd chosen not to. And now, when she slowly turned her gaze up to meet his and saw his eyes filled with genuine concern, she couldn't keep it to herself any longer.

"It's…it's my mother. She was supposed to come here tonight for dinner."

"Yeah. That's what you said. So where is she?"

"On her way to St. Louis."

"St. Louis? Why?"

"Because her no-good ex-husband decided he wanted to see her, so she went out to the airport on standby to see if she could get on a flight."

"She's leaving town instead of spending Christmas Eve with you?"

"Yeah. Looks that way."

"How could she do that to you?"

"How could she do it? She's a professional at doing it."

"What do you mean?"

"She missed my college graduation because some guy invited her to Cancun for the weekend. Does that tell you anything?"

Nick looked stunned. "Your mother did that?"

"Yeah. That and about a hundred other things over the years. But then she divorced that guy in St. Louis several months ago and moved here. Things were better. I thought sure she'd finally seen the light."

"What about your father? Where is he?"

She wiped her eyes. "The truth? I'm not even completely certain who my father is. There are three very good candidates, though."

Sara couldn't believe she'd just told Nick that. She gritted her teeth against the sob that rose in her throat.

He came closer. She held up her palm. "No. Don't."

"What?"

"Don't come near me."

He inched closer still. "Why not?"

"Because I'm not strong right now."

"You're about the strongest woman I know."

"Oh, yeah. I was a real paragon of strength when you were here the other night, wasn't I?"

Nick sighed. "Sara? Can I talk to you about that?"

"You've said plenty about it already."

"No. I haven't said nearly enough. I just wanted to tell you how sorry I am for what I did that night. I was out of line in about a hundred different ways. I pushed you into doing something I never should have. Strip chess? What the hell was I thinking?"

Sara blinked with surprise. Nick was apologizing? It stunned her so much she didn't know what to say.

"It wasn't all your fault," she told him. "I could have said no."

"Yes, but you shouldn't have had to. And I've felt terrible about it ever since. Yeah, I was mad when I left, but I had no right to be. It was my fault things happened the way they did."

"I was afraid you were going to talk about it on the air."

"I had no intention of doing that. I knew how much it would hurt you if I did." He reached into his pocket, pulled out the dimmer switch knob and handed it to her, shrugging weakly. "I know this was a really stupid excuse to see you, but when I found it in my pocket tonight…"

As she took the knob from him, he stepped closer, putting his hands on her upper arms and stroking them up and down. "I'm so sorry you're having such a bad night."

She closed her eyes. "Please don't do that."

"Why not?"

"Because I could fall for you, Nick. Right here, right now. And just the fact that I'm admitting that tells you I'm not in my right mind."

"Sara—"

"No," she said. "Don't be so nice to me. I can take you being a smart-ass. I can take sarcasm. I can take ego. But I can't take nice. So cut it out, will you?"

She tried to slip away from him, but he took hold of her arm and pulled her back. She put up a weak protest, but still he pulled her close and wrapped his arms around her. Then, before she knew it, she was putting her arms around him and resting her cheek against his shoulder and crying all over again. He just held her, moving his hand up and down her back in long, soothing strokes, and she was glad of it because he felt incredibly warm and solid and strong that suddenly everything that was so terrible about tonight didn't seem so terrible after all.

Finally, she sniffed a little and backed away. "You must think I'm a real mess."

"You're just disappointed. You decorated for Christmas, cooked dinner, the whole nine yards. And then suddenly your mother goes AWOL. You have good reason to be upset."

"I'm upset with myself, too," she said. "Why did I even get my hopes up?"

"That's easy. Because just once you wanted to have a nice, normal Christmas with a nice, normal mother. But it's not your fault she won't change. You just need to accept that fact and move on. Once you do, she can't hurt you anymore."

Sara groaned softly. "Will you stop being so damned insightful? You're making me feel like an amateur. And the last thing I need tonight is one more blow to my ego."

"Nah. This is just a little setback. Your ego's going to survive just fine."

Sara couldn't believe Nick had just told her the exact thing she told her clients time and time again. Why couldn't she take her own advice?

"Well," she said, suddenly feeling a little self-conscious. "I'm sure you have far better things to do tonight than stand here listening to me cry."

He sighed. "I guess I do have a party to go to."

"A party?"

"Yeah. My producer has one every year. They play all those Christmas parody songs and everybody drinks until they can't stand up. The only holiday glow anybody feels is through a bottle of beer. And I always play Santa Claus. You know. All the girls sit on my lap and tell me what they want for Christmas." He smiled briefly. "Bet that surprises you, doesn't it?"

"Yeah," she said. "That's a real shocker."

And still they stood there staring at each other.

"Well," Sara said, looking down at the knob she held. "I guess you have to go to your party. I mean, what's a party when the life of the party doesn't show up?"

Nick glanced toward the door, then turned back to gaze around her apartment, and she swore she saw a look of longing in his eyes.

"Sara?"

"Yes?"

"The party." He winced. "I swear if I have to listen to grandma getting run over by that reindeer one more time, I'm gonna go crazy."

A thought occurred to Sara, and her heart began to pound. She was on the verge of saying something she knew she shouldn't, because every moment she spent with Nick had the capacity to cause all kinds of problems. But tonight...just for tonight...

GET FREE BOOKS and a FREE GIFT WHEN YOU PLAY THE...

SLOT MACHINE GAME!

Just scratch off the silver box with a coin. Then check below to see the gifts you get!

DETACH AND MAIL CARD TODAY!

342 HDL D36E　　　　　　　　　　　**142 HDL D36U**

FIRST NAME　　　　　　　LAST NAME

ADDRESS

APT.#　　　　　　CITY

STATE/PROV.　　　　ZIP/POSTAL CODE

7	7	7	**Worth TWO FREE BOOKS plus a BONUS Mystery Gift!**
🍒	🍒	🍒	**Worth TWO FREE BOOKS!**
♣	♣	♣	**Worth ONE FREE BOOK!**
🔔	🔔	🍒	**TRY AGAIN!**

www.eHarlequin.com

(H-T-12/04)

The Harlequin Reader Service® — Here's how it works:

If offer card is missing write to: Harlequin Reader Service, 3010 Walden Ave., P.O. Box 1867, Buffalo NY 14240-1867

BUSINESS REPLY MAIL
FIRST-CLASS MAIL   PERMIT NO. 717-003   BUFFALO, NY

POSTAGE WILL BE PAID BY ADDRESSEE

HARLEQUIN READER SERVICE
3010 WALDEN AVE
PO BOX 1867
BUFFALO NY 14240-9952

NO POSTAGE
NECESSARY
IF MAILED
IN THE
UNITED STATES

"In that case," she said, "would you like to stay for dinner?"

Nick gave her one of those warm, wonderful smiles that quite simply took her breath away.

"I would *love* to stay for dinner."

10

SARA WENT INTO the kitchen to check on the turkey, and when she came back out to the living room, every bit of the holiday glow she'd turned off before Nick got there was blazing again—the fireplace, the candles and her Christmas tree. Everything that had seemed so bleak five minutes ago suddenly looked beautiful again.

Nick came into the kitchen, opened the bottle of wine she'd bought that afternoon and poured them both a glass. She took a sip, and it warmed her from the inside out. By the time they sat down to dinner, everything felt just...*perfect.*

"I'm not the world's best cook," Sara said. "Hopefully dinner will be okay."

"Are you kidding? This looks great. If you hadn't invited me to stay, do you know what I'd be eating right now?"

"What?"

"Beer and nachos. Now, Butch does add red and green peppers to the cheese sauce. After all, it's Christmas."

To Sara, the food didn't matter a bit, but the company did. As they ate, she discovered what a pleasure it was to be with a man who talked for a living, because there were never any of those awkward silences she often felt around other men. She remembered how Nick tried to draw her into conversation with him that first night they'd had dinner together and how much she'd resisted it.

Right now, she found that impossible to believe.

After dinner, Nick helped her clean up, and then they took the remainder of the wine and went into the living room. Sara sat down on the sofa. Nick took a seat beside her, resting his wineglass on his knee, seemingly unaware of the fact that if he so much as leaned a millimeter to his left, his thigh would be touching hers.

He turned slightly to face her, those brilliant blue eyes absolutely mesmerizing by the light of the fire. A smile spread slowly across his face.

"What?" she asked.

"This is nice."

"Yes. It is."

"Beats the hell out of pin the tail on the reindeer."

"What?"

"Never mind. You don't want to know." He took a deep breath and let it out slowly, and for a split second she felt his leg brush hers, a touch so minute it almost wasn't there, and yet she felt it. She picked up her wine. Took a sip. It was dangerous to drink more, she knew, but right now she didn't know any other way to calm herself down.

"Now I know why you wrote the book," Nick said.

"What?"

"Your mother."

Sara rested her wineglass on the table and sat back with a sigh. "You're being insightful again. Don't you ever let up?"

He smiled. "It's not that hard to deduce."

"Let's just say I've seen firsthand how some women screw up their lives with the wrong men."

"With a childhood like that, it must have been hard to get where you are now."

"I'm not where I am in spite of my mother. I'm there because of her. She set the example I was determined not to follow."

"Still, it must have been tough to do that on your own."

"I had some good people helping me along the way. My friend Karen, who you met, isn't just my publicist. We've known each other since high school. She had a bad home life, too, so we hung out together. It made all the difference to have somebody else around you could talk to who was going through the same stuff you were. And I had teachers along the way who recognized that I could move on the fast track, and they did a lot to help me out, too."

"So now that you're looking good professionally, what's next?"

"What do you mean?"

"Do you intend to get married?"

At the same time he asked the question, he moved his arm to the back of the sofa behind her head and faced her more directly, and she remembered something he said when he was here before: *You want a man who turns every molecule of his attention to you and makes you feel as if you're the only woman on earth.*

That was exactly how she felt right now.

"Married?" she said. "I don't know. I watched my mother screw it up three times. That'd scare anyone right out of matrimony." She paused, thinking about that. "But if I ever do get married, there'll be no second-guessing, no looking back. Till death do us part. Now, that may sound a little old-fashioned in a world where marriage has become pretty disposable. But that's the way I feel about it."

"I'm not knocking that point of view. My parents have been married for almost thirty-five years. That's the way it's supposed to work."

Given his reputation, she was surprised to hear him say

that. Then again, almost everything she'd learned about Nick had been a surprise.

"Where are you from?" she asked.

"Colorado Springs.

"Do your parents still live there?"

"Yeah. And my brother and his wife are still there, too. I was the only defector. I went from Tucson to Dallas to Chicago and finally back here, closer to home."

"It must be nice to be able to see your parents every once in a while."

"It is. As long as it's every once in a while."

"You don't get along?"

He smiled. "Oh, yeah. We do. I just wish they'd lighten up a little. You've never heard such nagging in your life."

"What do they nag about?"

"They think I should get a real job. And a real wife. And real children. And a real house in the suburbs. Just like my brother."

"What does your brother do for a living?"

"He's an investment banker. They *love* that."

"Ever consider settling down?"

"It's not in the cards for me just yet. I have things I want to do first."

"But still they nag."

"Oh, yeah. But it's nothing new. It was that way the entire time I was growing up. 'Nick, don't throw spiders on the girls. Nick, don't cut class to go snowboarding. Nick, don't jump off the roof with a towel tied around your neck and expect to fly.' I mean, how unreasonable can one set of parents get?"

"You actually jumped off a roof with a towel tied around your neck and thought you would *fly?*"

"Give me a break. I was five at the time."

"So you're the black sheep of the family."

"Nah. I'm just a little gray, leaning toward charcoal."

Sara smiled. She had a picture of his family in her mind already. He wasn't speaking with enough animosity to indicate a genuine problem there. They were probably just one of those families who wanted the best for him but got a little carried away when it came to expressing that.

"The older I get," Nick said, "the more tragic the expression on my mother's face gets. Pretty soon, she's going to start in with, 'Please, Nick, before I die...'"

Sara smiled. "Poor woman."

"Yeah. Poor *manipulative* woman." He gave Sara a look of mock disgust, then shrugged a little. "But in a way, I can't fault my parents for the way they feel. Conventional success would have come easily for me, and it killed them to see me pass it up. See, I was the smart one. I think my mother envisioned that she'd given birth to a future president of the United States. And a two-term one, at that. None of this being voted out after four years."

"But you had other plans."

"Yeah. I've always loved radio. It's my dream job. I actually get paid to talk to people. I know you're not real crazy about the content of my show, but believe it or not, it's pretty successful."

"I know it is. I've heard your statistics. You have a lot of listeners."

"Did I tell you it's on the verge of syndication?"

"Syndication? That's the big time."

"It's not a done deal yet, but it's looking good."

"Congratulations. Do your parents know about this?"

"I'm going to tell them tomorrow. I'm driving to Colorado Springs in the morning. I'll stay over tomorrow night, and then drive back on the twenty-sixth."

Sara smiled. "That must be nice."

"What?"

"To have a family waiting for you on Christmas Day. I know you say they nag you a lot, but still…it must be nice."

Nick nodded and took another sip of wine. After a moment, he turned to her. "So do you have any plans for tomorrow?"

"No. Not really."

He stared at her oddly.

"What?"

"Come with me."

Sara was shocked. "What?"

"Yeah. Come with me. It'll be fun. My mother will assume you're my girlfriend. She'll be ecstatic."

"Nick, I'm not your girlfriend."

"And there's not really a Santa Claus, either, but Christmas is a great time for make-believe. Nobody's hurt. You get a great Christmas dinner, I get my family off my back for a few blessed hours. Everybody's happy."

"You're serious."

"Of course I am."

"You're just pitying me because I'm going to be alone."

"Nope. I'm way too selfish for that. I'm pitying *me*. You can be a nice little buffer between me and my family."

"But you said you were staying there overnight. I can't do that."

"Why can't you?"

"I don't even know your family."

"Doesn't matter. There's plenty of room."

"You want me to crash your family gathering on Christmas Day?"

"Are you kidding? One look at you, and my parents will roll out the red carpet. They're getting on in years, Sara.

Don't deny them this tiny bit of hope that their wayward son might actually marry a nice girl some day."

"I'm not sure we should be seen together. If people think there's something going on between us—"

"Colorado Springs is a hundred miles from here. We don't have to worry about that."

"If somebody even sees us in a car together—"

"How will they know who you are?"

"My photo's on my book jacket."

"Okay, but what are the odds of somebody knowing what both of us look like and putting us together?"

He was right. The odds were pretty slim. "But me staying with your family? Come on, Nick. You've got to admit that's a little strange."

"Nah. It'll be fun. In spite of their nagging, my parents aren't uptight, and they love guests. And you can throw around a bunch of psychology talk. They'll love that."

Sara couldn't believe this. It felt so strange—Nick Chandler asking her to go with him to his family gathering on Christmas Day? That concept was hard enough to hold in her mind, much less act on.

Still, tonight Nick had turned an evening that could have been one of the worst ones of her life into one of the best. She owed him for that. And he was looking at her with such hope...

"Okay," she said. "I'll come."

He grinned. "This is gonna be *great*. For once, I can enjoy Christmas without my mother giving me the sad, pitiful face."

"You're absolutely sure it'll be okay?"

"It'll be better than okay. Trust me. I'll call my mom tonight and let her know you're coming with me." Nick glanced at his watch, then blew out a breath. "And now I really do have to be going. I left a friend at that party and told him I'd be back to pick him up."

They stood up and she followed him to the front door.

"I was planning on leaving about eight in the morning," Nick said. "Does that work for you?"

"That's fine."

"Good. I'll pick you up then."

"Now, I'm not lying to your family about being your girlfriend," Sara said. "We'll just say we're friends."

"It won't matter what we say. They'll make all the flying leaps of logic necessary to convince themselves that we're a couple. We'll just play along, and everyone will be happy."

Sara sighed. "I'm afraid I was never much good at make-believe."

"Why not?"

"Let's put it this way. While you were busy jumping off your roof trying to fly, I was wondering who all those guys were who were hopping in and out of my mother's bed."

"Well, then, why don't I show you how it's done?"

"What?"

"Come with me."

He led her to the kitchen doorway, where he stopped, took her by the shoulders and stood her beneath it.

"Nick? What are you doing?"

He pointed to the top of the door frame. "Look up there."

She looked up. "What?"

"Don't you see it?"

"See what?"

"It's as plain as day."

"I don't see anything."

"That's because you have to use your imagination. It's

hanging right there above the doorway. Small green leaves, little white berries…"

For a moment, she actually wondered why he was pointing at something that clearly wasn't there. Then light dawned, and she met his gaze again.

"Mistletoe?" she whispered.

He smiled softly. "See? There's nothing wrong with your imagination at all."

With his gaze fixed on hers, he slowly lifted his hands to rest them on her shoulders, and his gaze drifted down to her lips. She couldn't believe it.

He was going to kiss her.

As he leaned in slowly, she watched the descent of his lips toward hers, knowing she should object, because this was exactly the kind of thing that could get her into a whole lot of trouble where Nick was concerned. After all, hadn't Karen warned her to stay as far away from him as possible?

But she couldn't help it. This was Christmas Eve, she was standing beneath the most beautiful imaginary mistletoe she'd ever seen, on the verge of being kissed by the most attractive man she'd ever met, and she just didn't want to break the spell.

For a moment Nick hovered so close she could feel his warm breath, and then he closed his lips over hers. She rested her hand against his chest, tilting her head so their lips fell together perfectly. Time seemed to slow to a crawl, every second passing like years. As wild and exciting as his kiss had been a few nights ago, that was how warm and gentle it was now. Any lingering mistrust she had in him seemed to fade away, and the place in her heart that had been so cold only a few hours ago was filled with warmth.

Finally, he pulled away, taking a deep breath and letting

it out slowly. "No apologies for this one," he murmured. "The mistletoe made me do it."

"Holiday magic?"

"Yeah. I hear it makes people do all kinds of crazy things."

His hands flexed against her shoulders, his gaze playing over her face, and her heart jolted with the realization that he was thinking of asking for more than a single kiss. Maybe a lot more.

But then he took a slow step backward, his hands falling away from her. "I'd better go."

Sara felt the strangest combination of relief and disappointment. Every molecule in her body hummed with the desire to throw good sense out the window, say to hell with the consequences and just go wild for once in her life. But Nick was clearly the wrong man. Wrong in so many ways that she couldn't even count them. But for some reason, on this night, he felt more right for her than any man she'd ever known.

She followed him to the door and handed him his coat. As he put it on, she folded her arms and looked up at him, speaking softly. "Thanks for returning the knob."

"No problem."

"I'll be here at eight in the morning," he said.

"I'll be waiting."

She opened the door to a burst of cold wind, and Nick slipped outside and walked to his car. She closed the door behind him, then peeked out the window beside the door, watching until he drove away.

Sara let the curtain fall back to the window, then blew out the candles and turned off the lights. Walking into her bedroom, she slipped into a nightshirt and lay down in bed.

She'd get up early tomorrow and pack a few things, but

right now all she wanted to do was soak up a little more of the feeling Nick had left her with. Whatever small connection they'd found tonight could lead to nothing else—they both knew that—but for now, she wanted to lie awake for a while and imagine that it could.

11

IT WAS A DAZZLING Christmas morning, with bright sunlight reflecting off the snow-covered mountains, their peaks sharp and clear in the crisp morning air. Nick was relaxing in the driver's seat of his SUV, one arm leaning on the console and his other wrist looped over the steering wheel. He wore a pair of sunglasses, a Denver Broncos sweatshirt over a pair of worn jeans and an expression of total relaxation.

It struck Sara how different he was from other men she'd known, who sat up straight with their hands at ten and two o'clock and approached driving on snow-covered roads with the utmost seriousness. Nick, on the other hand, always gave the impression that he was in control of everything but that nothing was a big deal. In Sara's life, where so many things had been *very* big deals, just being in the same car with him made her feel calm and tranquil and totally stress-free.

Unfortunately, that feeling came to an abrupt halt the moment they entered the city limits of Colorado Springs.

Nick glanced at her. "You're nervous."

"A little."

"No need to be."

"What did you tell your mother about me?"

"That you're a highly educated psychologist who plays a mean game of chess."

Sara raised an eyebrow. "Did you tell her what kind of chess?"

"And give the poor woman a heart attack?"

They drove down the state highway a few more miles. Then Nick slowed the car and turned onto a narrow black-top road lined with towering pine trees.

"They don't live in town?" Sara asked.

"Just north of town." He pointed ahead. "And just around the next corner."

The lane curved sharply, and when the house came into view, Sara's mouth fell open.

It was big. No, not big. *Huge.* Two stories, with tall white columns, sprawling in front of a hilly landscape set against acre after acre of snow-covered aspens.

"That's some house," she said.

Nick just shrugged.

"Most of the professors I know aren't exactly wealthy."

"My father's an economics professor. He knows a thing or two about investing."

"And your mother?"

"She teaches medieval literature and doesn't know the first thing about investing. She does, however, make a hell of a pecan pie."

Nick brought his car to a halt in the driveway. The front door opened immediately and an older man and woman came to the car. The resemblance between Nick and his father was striking—the same blue eyes, the same dark hair, only his father's was graying at the temples and he wore wire-rimmed glasses. His mother, on the other hand, was short and stout with light brown hair, looking every bit the professor of medieval literature Nick had said she was.

They got out of the car. Nick gave his parents a hug, then introduced them as Richard and Anna.

"Sara! We're so glad you're here!" Anna said brightly. "Nick has told us all about you."

As Anna ushered her toward the house, Nick and his father grabbed their bags and the Christmas presents Nick had brought. They stepped into the entry, and Sara saw that while it was a large house, it was cozy at the same time, with the kind of warmth that made a house a home. The banister curving toward the second floor was draped with pine garland and bows, and when Sara glimpsed into the family room she saw a Christmas tree that had to be at least ten feet tall.

Anna turned to Nick. "I made up your old room for Sara. That way, she'll have a private bath. Show her upstairs, and then when you come back down, Brent and Lori should be here, and we can have brunch."

"Thanks, Mom." Nick grabbed Sara's bag and led her up the stairs. He opened the door to one of the rooms, which was decorated in the same homey style as the rest of the house.

"Lace curtains and a floral comforter," Sara said. "I assume your mother has redecorated since you were a teenager?"

"Yeah, there was something about black lights, death metal posters and quad speakers that just didn't fit her image of a guest room." He put Sara's bag on the bed.

"I like your parents. They're really nice."

"See, I told you it wouldn't feel weird."

Just then, Sara heard a car door. She went to the window and saw a white Lexus in the driveway. "Brent and Lori?"

Nick came up beside her. "Yeah."

"Hmm. Nice car."

"Brent wouldn't be seen in anything less."

"A bit of a status seeker?"

"Let's just say he likes the trappings of success." He

turned away from the window. "We'd better get back downstairs. It looks as if my mother wants to feed us."

"I've already had breakfast."

"You can try that argument. It won't get you anywhere, but you can try it."

Sara and Nick went back down the stairs, meeting Brent and Lori as they came through the front door. The family resemblance had carried over to Brent, too, but his eyes were green and his hair close-cropped, and he wore a pair of slacks and a sweater that Sara was pretty sure was cashmere. His wife, Lori, was a cute little blonde who looked to be about six months pregnant.

"Merry Christmas!" Lori gave Anna and Richard big hugs, then turned and smiled at Sara. "Well. You must be Sara."

"Sara," Nick said, "this is my brother, Brent, and his wife, Lori."

"Anna phoned this morning to tell us about you," Lori said to Sara. "We're so glad you decided to come."

"I'm happy to be here," Sara said, taking an instant liking to Nick's sister-in-law. His brother she wasn't so sure about. He was staring at her as if she were a bug under a magnifying glass.

"Mom told us you have a doctorate in psychology," Brent said to Sara. "Is that true?"

"Yes, it is. I'm in private practice in Boulder."

His gaze narrowed. "Interesting. Where did you and Nick meet?"

Uh-oh. The last thing she wanted to tell them was that he had interviewed her on his show, because then she'd have to say why he interviewed her, and that would lead to her telling them about the book she'd written, and…

And she didn't want to go there at all. But before she could fabricate an answer, Nick spoke up.

"We have a mutual friend," he said. "Karen Dawson. She introduced us."

Sara winced at Nick's excessive stretching of the truth. "But we're really just friends," she added quickly.

"Oh," Brent said, with an expression that said, *Thank God. Finally this makes sense.*

"Actually," Nick said, "we're good friends." He turned to wink at Sara. "*Very* good friends."

Damn. She should have known Nick would do this. Just because he'd promised he wouldn't say outright that she was his girlfriend didn't mean he wouldn't find a hundred ways to imply it.

Brent looked back and forth between them in disbelief, and it made Sara very uncomfortable. When he and Lori followed Nick's parents into the dining room, Sara hung back, grabbing Nick's arm.

"What's the matter?" he asked.

"I don't think your brother likes me," she whispered.

"Oh, no," Nick whispered back. "He likes you a lot. That's the problem."

"What?"

"It freaks him out to see me with a woman like you."

"A woman like me?"

"You know. Natural hair color. Natural fingernails. Natural—" He flicked his gaze to Sara's breasts, then gave her a smile. "Well, you get the picture. And that's driving him nuts."

"I don't get it."

"See, he's the shining son. The overachiever. The successful one. By bringing you here, I've screwed up the normal order of things. It's classic sibling rivalry, Dr. Davenport."

"So he feels threatened by you."

"Yes."

"Because I'm here?"

"Oh, yeah. I'm supposed to date women who don't know what Ph.D. means, much less have one. What's my brother going to do if I get serious about a woman like you? What if you lead me down the path of normalcy and I become a lawyer or a stock broker or something? What if—God forbid—we were to get married and have children and suddenly I'm not an aimless slacker anymore? I just might knock him off his perch."

"But none of that is going to happen."

Nick grinned. "Yeah, but he doesn't know that. Throw in my potential syndication deal, and I can really mess with his mind. I don't get the opportunity to get under my brother's skin very often. This is going to be fun."

Sara felt a twinge of panic. "Nick, don't you dare do anything embarrassing."

"Don't worry. My family's used to me by now."

"I meant don't do anything to embarrass *me*."

He grinned. "Relax. Just have fun with it, okay?"

With that, he took her by the hand and led her into the dining room, a gesture that was a little too personal for just friends, but with his family watching, she couldn't jerk away her hand.

What had been the matter with her last night? What had made her agree to come here today? This was insane. Nick lived to rattle cages, upset applecarts and shake up the status quo, and she'd agreed to leap right into the middle of the action.

Nick pulled out Sara's chair, then sat down next to her at the table. His mother started passing around a plate of Danishes and croissants.

"So, Nick," Brent said, as he filled his plate, "I guess you're still playing the radio game, huh?"

"Yeah, Brent. I'm still playing the radio game. I take it all is going well in the world of high finance?"

"Of course. Don't believe all those dire economic warnings you keep hearing. They don't apply to investors who know what they're doing."

"Brent just got another promotion," their mother said. "The second one in two years."

"Congratulations," Nick said.

"I finished my M.B.A.," Brent said. "That was what did it. The big bosses love higher education."

"You know, Nick," his father said, "you might consider going back and finishing that undergrad degree. You could transfer what credits you have to the University of Colorado."

"Yeah, Dad. I know. But the thing is, I have this job I really like that pays the bills. I'm thinking all that going to class would get in the way of that."

"Yes, I know it would be inconvenient, but a good education is worth anything you have to do to get it."

"Your father just thinks that now that you're older, you should be thinking about settling down," Anna said. "Getting a job that's a little more…stable."

"Actually, Mom, Mercury Media has approached me about taking my show into syndication. If the deal goes through, pretty soon you're going to be able to hear it all over the country. It doesn't get much more stable than that."

Silence fell over the table. No rattling of silverware. No clinking of glasses. No comments from Brent designed to put Nick down and elevate himself.

Nothing.

Finally, his father broke the silence. "Syndication? Well. That's impressive."

"Yeah. They'd probably move me into a dozen new markets at first, then go from there."

"That must mean your show is pretty successful."

"Yeah, Dad. It is."

"That's wonderful, Nick," Anna said. Then she lowered her voice, a hopeful look entering her eyes. "Does this mean you won't be interviewing any more of *those* women?"

"Afraid not, Mom. It means I'll probably be interviewing even more of *those* women."

"Syndication?" Brent said. "With *that* kind of programming?"

"If it didn't have *that* kind of programming," Nick said, "it wouldn't be moving into syndication."

"Well, at least you might make some real money. What are the odds of it coming through?"

"They're still talking. But my agent seems to think it's all but a done deal."

Brent looked surprised. "You have an agent?"

"Yeah, Brent. That's how these deals are handled."

"Well," Nick's brother said offhandedly, "I guess if you have to stay a frat boy forever, at least you'll be well-paid to do it."

Ah, Sara thought. A cheap shot. That, along with Brent's tense posture and his guarded expression, said he really did feel threatened that his brother might finally be making good. She flicked her gaze to Nick, wondering how he'd feel about the insult, only to find that his smile had grown even bigger.

"Yep," Nick said, "and there's a big advantage to being a well-paid frat boy."

"What's that?"

"All of the money and none of the responsibility."

"Oh, yeah?" Brent looked at Sara. "So what do you think about that 'no responsibility' part?"

All eyes went to Sara, and she paused for a moment, wondering what to say. "Uh…my opinion really doesn't matter. What Nick does with his career is his own business."

"An understanding woman," Brent said to Nick. "Given what you do, you could sure use one of those. I guess it's too bad you're just friends, huh?"

Nick turned to Sara, sliding his arm across the back of her chair. "I already told you, Brent. We're not just friends. We're *very good* friends."

And then he leaned in and kissed her.

When Nick's lips met Sara's, she was so shocked that she froze in disbelief. It wasn't a prolonged kiss, but it was more than a peck on the lips, just enough take them out of the realm of friends and into the realm of relationship. And Sara wanted to kill him. What was she supposed to do now?

As Nick pulled away, out of the corner of her eye, she saw Brent's dumbfounded expression, Lori's grin of delight, Richard's raised eyebrows and Anna's beaming smile.

"Brunch looks great, Mom," Nick said. "Somebody want to pass me those eggs?"

12

AFTER BRUNCH, Anna shooed Sara and Nick into the family room, saying Sara was a guest so she wasn't allowed to do dishes. That was fine by Sara, because it gave her an opportunity to have a word with Nick. Or several words. Several pointed, admonishing words, which he was going to listen to or *else.*

The moment they sat down on the sofa, she turned to him. "Why did you do that?"

"Do what?"

"Kiss me in front of your family!"

He shrugged. "I don't know. It just seemed like the right thing to do at the time."

"*Friends* don't kiss like that!"

"So you were embarrassed?"

"Yes!"

"Oh." He looked solemn for a moment. "You know, if I do it a couple more times, maybe the embarrassment will fade."

"You're using me, Nick. You want to get back at your brother, so—"

"Now, wait a minute. You think that's the only reason I did it? Because it irritates the hell out of Brent to see me kissing a smart, beautiful professional woman who could have any man she wants, but for some unknown reason she's having a relationship with me?"

Sara blinked with confusion. Nick positively tied her brain into knots sometimes. Only he could come back with a response that was all wound up in a compliment, making it impossible for her to respond.

"Or," Nick said, "do you think maybe I did it because I'll use any excuse I can get to kiss that smart, beautiful professional woman no matter who happens to be around?"

His voice had dropped into a lower range, becoming sultry and provocative, his eyes locked on to hers. A strand of hair had fallen along her cheek, and he caught it with his forefinger and tucked it behind her ear. Just that tiny touch, his fingertip dragging along her skin, sent sparks of sensation racing through her.

She turned away suddenly. "Don't do that."

"Why not?"

"For the same reason I don't want you kissing me."

"Because you like it and you don't want to admit it?"

"No. Because it's totally inappropriate in front of your family. Because I'm not your girlfriend. Because nothing can ever happen between us, so we shouldn't even be going there. Do *not* kiss me again."

"Can't promise that."

"I'm not joking, Nick."

He sighed.

"I mean it. Promise me you won't do it again."

"Okay, okay." He rolled his eyes. "I promise not to kiss you again."

"Thank you."

Sara felt a bit of relief, even though she held out little hope that Nick had any intention of keeping his word about that.

Later, the family exchanged gifts, and in the early afternoon, Anna fixed a light snack in anticipation of Christmas dinner that night. Then Nick surprised Sara by asking his mother to bring out a family photo album.

Since flipping through family pictures wasn't an activity most men went out of their way to be subjected to, Sara wondered what he was up to. Then Nick suggested that Anna sit on the loveseat on the other side of Sara. It was a big loveseat, but not *that* big, and suddenly she was pressed against Nick from her hip to her thigh to her knee.

As Anna opened the album and set it on Sara's lap, Nick put his arm across the back of the sofa behind Sara's head. Her heart skipped a little, then skipped again as he leaned closer to her, their legs pressed even more tightly together, as if he wanted a better look at the album.

What was he *doing?*

Nick dropped his hand from the back of the sofa and began rubbing his thumb back and forth against her upper arm. A sharp tingle raced through her that made her stomach quiver and goose bumps rise on her arm. Anna kept talking, but suddenly Sara wasn't comprehending a word she said, her mind blanking to everything around her except Nick. Since his family already thought she was his girlfriend, nobody seemed to think anything about how familiar and personal his touch was.

Sara couldn't think about anything else.

When Anna finally closed the album, Sara readied herself to scoot away from Nick at the first available moment, but he spoke up first.

"Hey, Mom. Aren't there a few more albums in the hall closet?"

Sara flicked her gaze to Anna, who looked at Nick admonishingly. "No. That was enough. Any more would bore Sara to tears."

"Aw, come on. She's not bored. Are you, Sara?"

Oh, *great*. What was she supposed to say to that? She smiled sweetly at Nick. "No. Of course not. I'd love to see more."

Anna rose from the loveseat. "Richard, come with me. I can't reach that shelf in the closet."

As Richard and Anna disappeared down the hall, Brent and Lori headed to the kitchen for something to drink. Sara tried to move away from Nick, but he tightened his arm around her.

"Better stay put," he said. "My mother will be back in just a minute."

"Nick? What are you doing?"

"Hey, I've kept my promise, haven't I? I haven't kissed you once. I'd say that shows remarkable self-control on my part."

"Self-control? Are you kidding? You've done everything under the sun *but* kiss me."

He glanced at her lips. "Are you sure those are off-limits?"

"Yes. And so is the rest of me. So would you please—"

"Sorry. I'm invoking the five-second rule."

"What?"

"You didn't object to me touching you within five seconds, so now you've lost the right."

"But your family was here. What did you want me to do? Slap your hand away?"

"Of course not. I wanted you to touch me, too."

Nick picked up her hand and placed it on his thigh, closing his palm over it. Sara opened her mouth to object, but the feel of hard muscle beneath soft denim made that protest stick in her throat.

"Let's just enjoy our time together," he murmured, stroking her hand. "What can it hurt?"

In spite of the fact that he'd choreographed this situation, he was looking at her with a remarkable lack of guile, and she found her resolve crumbling. It wasn't as if she hated sitting here with him like this. In fact, it was nice. *Really* nice. She hadn't had much of a family life growing up, so being here with him felt good. And no matter how much she protested, every time he touched her it made her feel even better.

"Besides," Nick said, "if we go through all the albums, eventually you'll see some great shots of me naked."

"What?"

"Okay, so I was six months old at the time. But I was pretty damned good-looking even back then."

"Did anyone ever tell you your ego arrives about five minutes before you do?"

"It runs in the family. You did meet my brother, right?"

"You know, you were right about Brent. He does seem threatened by you."

Nick smiled. "So you noticed?"

"As you said. Classic sibling rivalry."

His smile faded. "Even though I've always told myself that I don't care what my family thinks, just once I'd like to be the one to pull off something big. My parents are respected professors—department heads, tenure, the whole nine yards. My brother is a hotshot investment banker who handles all kinds of big mergers and millions of dollars' worth of assets. And what do I do? I interview strippers."

She smiled. "You interviewed me, didn't you?"

"You're the one tiny glimmer of class my program has ever seen." He sighed. "I don't expect that my family will ever be happy with the content of my show, but they do know success when they see it, no matter what field we're talking about. This syndication deal is my one shot at the big time. It's going to happen, Sara. No matter what I have to do."

All at once, Sara realized that even though Nick seemed to take nothing in his life seriously, he was far from the slacker his brother thought he was. And while she had to agree with his family that the content of his show was a little questionable, she admired his single-mindedness in going after the things he wanted.

Just then, Anna and Richard came back into the room with more photo albums. "Here we go!" Anna said placing one of them in Sara's lap. "Disney World 1984."

"Oh, good," Nick said, grinning. "That was a nice, long trip. Lots and *lots* of photos. Let's see…then there was the Caribbean cruise in 1985, Yellowstone in 1986—"

Sara gave Nick's leg a hard but furtive squeeze. He widened his eyes a little in a mock expression of pain only she would notice, then took her hand, presumably to ward off future reprimands. When he started rubbing his thumb along the top of it in a slow, mesmerizing motion, pretty soon the last thing Sara was thinking about was the photos of the Chandler family's foray into Disney's Adventureland.

Face it, Sara. You're happy to have an excuse to touch him, too.

"Five-second rule," Nick whispered, so softly only she could hear.

As if she'd considered pulling away.

As Anna talked, flipping album pages and describing the photos, Sara barely heard her. She was too busy absorbing every nuance of Nick, from his warm, masculine smell, to his rich, resonant voice, to the nerve-awakening sensation of his skin against hers. Every tiny move either of them made seemed magnified a thousand times, until Sara couldn't sense anything around her except him. Suddenly, she was caught up in the most amazing feeling, one she couldn't have imagined before. This seemed normal, as if being here with Nick was the most natural thing in the world. Closing her eyes for a moment, she savored the feeling, wanting to remember it, because when tomorrow came, all this would have to come to an end.

Later they had dinner, then gathered around the television for a Chandler family tradition: watching football. Or, rather, everyone else watched football.

Sara watched Nick.

As he and his family cheered at the good plays and groaned at the bad ones, she took the opportunity to steal glances at Nick, amazed at just how animated and alive he was, so different from the serious, conservative men she was used to being around who might watch a football game but wouldn't be caught dead yelling at a referee. She'd always thought that indicated maturity and level-headedness, but now she was beginning to realize Nick had something those men didn't: the willingness to let go and have a good time. And she'd never imagined just how appealing that could be.

It was ten o'clock that night before Anna and Richard finally rose and said they were going to bed, and Brent and Lori decided they'd turn in, too. Nick and Sara stood up to say goodnight, watching as the four of them went up the stairs.

Then they were alone together.

"I thought they'd never go to bed," Nick said.

"It's late," Sara said. "I suppose I should go to bed, too."

"No way. I've waited all day to be alone with you." To her surprise, he pulled her right up next to him, lacing his arms around her. Her heart thumped wildly.

"Nick? What are you doing?"

"You know how I promised I wouldn't kiss you?"

"Yes?"

"I can only be good for so long."

He dropped his lips against hers in a wild, scorching kiss, as if he were unleashing every bit of the frustration he'd felt all day because kissing her had been off-limits. It seemed to go on endlessly, until she felt as if her bones were liquefying and she was dissolving in his arms.

Finally he pulled back, his breath warm against her lips. "Come to my room with me."

"*What?*"

"My room is downstairs, and all the others are upstairs. No one will know."

"I can't do that!"

"I don't want this night to end. I want to see more of you." He touched his lips to hers. "All of you."

Sara was stunned. "Wh-what are you saying?"

"I know this can't go anywhere. If people found out you had any kind of relationship with me, your credibility would be shot. But just for tonight..." He paused, his eyes filled with desire. "Let me make love to you."

His words excited her and shocked her all at the same time, and for a moment she was speechless. All day long, every one of Nick's glances had lingered a little longer than the one before it, with every touch a little more intimate than the last. But still she couldn't have imagined...

"No," she said. "That's crazy. This is your parents' house."

"And if we were someplace else?"

"It wouldn't matter. We can't do this."

"This is our last chance. Once we're back in Boulder, we can never see each other again."

"Nick, please—"

"This has been killing me all day, Sara. I want you. And I know you want me, too."

"Don't you understand? What I *want* isn't the issue!"

"Then you do want me?"

Of course she wanted him. She had almost from the first moment she met him, and spending this day with him had only strengthened that feeling and made resisting him nearly impossible.

"It doesn't matter what I want," she said. "It's the wrong thing to do."

She turned to leave the room. He reached for her, but she slipped from his grasp. She made it halfway to the stairs before he caught her arm again.

"Sara. Wait."

She stopped, squeezing her eyes closed with frustration.

"Until the sun comes up tomorrow," he said quietly, "you can always change your mind. My room is the second door on the left. And you can bet I'll be awake. Just knowing you're in the same house will probably keep me up all night."

She pulled away again and made it to the stairs. Her hand on the banister, she wavered for a moment, unable to resist glancing back at him. And she couldn't believe what she saw.

Hanging on the door frame above his head was a sprig of mistletoe.

Good Lord. He looked tempting enough already, and he was standing under *mistletoe*? Sara felt as if fate had handed her an engraved invitation to walk back to him, wrap her arms around his neck and kiss him, and it took every bit of self-control she had to keep from doing exactly that.

"You'd better get some sleep, Nick," she told him. "I'll see you in the morning."

She hated the way her words sounded, so dull and final, but still she turned and climbed the stairs, knowing he was watching her and resisting the urge to look back one more time. She went into her bedroom and leaned against the closed door, taking several deep breaths and telling herself over and over that she'd done the right thing.

Later, she lay awake in bed, staring at the moonlight casting shadows on the wall, imagining Nick in bed downstairs. She wondered if he really was lying awake thinking about her, just as she was thinking about him. But she was insane even to think about taking him up on his offer. It would be one thing to say goodbye to Nick. It would be another thing entirely to say goodbye to him the morning after they'd made love.

Sara rolled over and pulled the covers up over her shoulder. With a deep, calming breath, she closed her eyes and tried to sleep.

Impossible.

Once we're back in Boulder, we can never see each other again.

Just the thought of that filled her with remorse. Saying goodbye after making love might be painful, but what about the pain of regret she would feel if she passed up the opportunity to be with a fun, sexy, spontaneous man like Nick, if only for one night?

Her eyes sprang open. *Do it.*

Those two tiny words pounded in her mind, growing in magnitude with every breath she took.

No. She couldn't.

But this is your last chance. After tomorrow, he'll be gone for good.

She froze for several seconds, letting the memory of Nick's talented hands and his incredible kisses wash over her. Suddenly she couldn't bear the thought that he may already have touched her for the last time. An unaccustomed feeling of recklessness rose inside her, driving her to sit up and flip on the lamp.

He wants you. You want him. So what are you waiting for?

Driven by a surge of sheer desire, Sara tossed off the covers, grabbed her robe and threw it on. Before any second thoughts could take hold, she carefully opened her bedroom door and peeked into the hall. It was deserted. She hurried out of the room and down the stairs, then passed through the family room to the short hall that led to the bedrooms, her bare feet moving silently on the hardwood floors.

She found the right door and knocked softly. Only a few seconds passed before it opened. Nick wore nothing but a pair of pajama pants and a look of surprise.

"Sara?" he said. "Does this mean—"

Before he could say another word, she wrapped her arms around his neck, pulled him down to her and kissed him.

13

NICK GAVE a start of surprise, but Sara never let up. She kissed him with every ounce of passion she had, using her lips, her tongue, her hands, her body, trying to tell him that he wasn't alone, to let him know just how frustrated she'd felt all day long from wanting him so much.

Finally, their kiss wound down from hot and urgent to warm and dreamy, until Sara felt as if she were floating a foot above the ground. Her arms still wrapped around his neck, she eased her lips away from his.

"It can only be tonight, Sara. That's all. We both know that."

"Then we'd better make the most of it, hadn't we?"

The look in Nick's eyes when she said that absolutely set her on fire. He dived in for another kiss, shoving her robe aside and skimming his hand along her hip, bunching up the tail of her nightshirt, then sliding his hand beneath it until it met her bare thigh. A soft moan of satisfaction rose in his throat.

"You feel so good, Sara," he whispered against her lips. "All soft and warm and…" He exhaled. "Just *perfect*."

He wrapped his hand around her thigh and pulled her against him until she felt his erection pressing against her abdomen, and the evidence of just how much he wanted her made her want him that much more. He unfastened her robe and pushed it off her shoulders, letting it fall to the floor behind her.

Then suddenly it dawned on her what she was wearing, and she felt a flush of embarrassment.

"Damn," she whispered.

"What's wrong?"

She closed her eyes. Her favorite flannel nightshirt was soft and comfy and threadbare and about as sexy as a pair of overalls. "I just realized what I'm wearing."

"What's the matter with it?"

"It's old and ugly and *flannel*, that's what's the matter."

He leaned away, looking down at her. "My God, you're right!" he whispered. "I hadn't noticed that! I'd better get that ugly old thing off you as fast as I can!"

Sara couldn't help smiling. "You just refuse to let me take myself seriously, don't you?"

"No fun in that," Nick said, unfastening one button of the nightshirt, then another. "And for the record, I don't give a damn what you're wearing as long as it eventually ends up on the floor."

He unbuttoned another button, then surprised her by growing impatient and simply pulling it off over her head. He tossed it aside, and when he looked back his gaze fell on her breasts. He froze, staring at them for what seemed like an eternity, and Sara got the distinct impression that he didn't like what he saw.

She turned and reached for the lamp. Nick caught her arm. "Nope. Leave it on."

Sara felt a twinge of apprehension. She'd never made love with the lights on before. She'd always imagined that every imperfection would be magnified tenfold, and she had plenty that had no business being magnified.

Nick backed away a step and pulled off his shirt, then

coaxed her to lie on the bed. As he sat down beside her, he was staring down at her again. Self-consciousness finally overtook her and she folded her arms over her breasts. He caught her wrists and eased her hands down to her sides.

"No, sweetheart. Don't do that."

"You're staring."

"Why do you think I'm staring?"

"I'm not sure, since there's not much to look at."

"Ah, you think just because they're small, there's nothing to interest a man?"

"So it goes sometimes."

"I'm interested, Sara. Believe me."

Still holding her wrists at her sides, he leaned in and pressed his lips to the upper slope of one breast, then the other. He flicked one nipple with his tongue. She stifled a gasp and squirmed against him, but he held her wrists gently to the bed as he continued to tease her nipple with soft strokes of his tongue. The too-intense feeling soon melted into pleasure, then need, and she arched up against him, wanting more. Finally he closed his mouth over her nipple and sucked, causing a whole new kind of pleasure that was almost too exquisite to bear. He moved to her other breast and gave it the same treatment, kissing and licking and sucking until she thought she'd go out of her mind. Then he moved up and kissed her neck, whispering in her ear.

"I think you're beautiful, Sara, or I wouldn't want you so damned much. Don't hide anything from me."

He eased away and released her wrists, only to loop his fingers into the edge of her panties and pull them down. Tossing them aside, he stood up, got rid of his pants, then lay down beside her again. As he leaned in to kiss her, he put his hand on her abdomen, then slipped it down between her legs. She automatically let her knee drop to one side, and he eased his fingers inside her, humming his approval when he felt how hot and ready for him she was.

"Tell me, sweetheart," he whispered in her ear. "Orgasm. Is it easy for you or not?"

She felt a flush of embarrassment at the question. She'd certainly never had a man ask her that. But Nick was stroking her so softly, kissing her neck, coaxing an answer out of her, until finally she told him the truth.

"Sometimes it happens," she whispered back, "and sometimes it doesn't." She paused. "Mostly it doesn't."

"We'll see about that."

He rolled off the bed, grabbed his pants, and she realized he was pulling out a condom. He tore the package open and rolled it on, then lay on his back on the bed and pulled her on top of him, urging her to sit astride him. Suddenly she realized that he wanted it like this, and it made her a little nervous. As embarrassing as it was to admit even to herself, her mundane sex life had never resulted in anything remotely adventurous, even something as commonplace as this. But Nick was holding on to her hips and guiding her to him, and she assumed it had to be a pretty straightforward thing to do. But when she tried to take him inside, he shifted his body until she simply glided over him.

A little frustrated, she tried to take him again, only to have him shift one more time and move her back and forth instead. Back and forth. Over and over. She was soft and wet and he was rock-hard and ready, and the combination of the two rubbing together felt…good. But still she didn't understand it. How was this supposed to be good for either of them?

A few moments later, she found out.

To her surprise, the combination of continuous motion and pressure in exactly the right place set off a spark of sensation. Seconds later, that spark ignited, and the heat it created built with every stroke. Caught up in the feeling, she rested her hands on Nick's shoulders and continued what he'd started, sliding back and forth along the length of him, putting direct pressure exactly where she needed it the most.

Nick let go of her hips and cupped her breasts, squeezing and releasing, strumming her nipples with his thumbs, sending hot streaks of sensation right down between her legs. She opened her eyes to find him staring up at her, watching every nuance of her expression, and she had the most uncanny feeling that he knew her body better than she knew it herself.

She moved faster. Pressed down harder. As she glided back and forth on top of him, her breathing became hot and ragged and she almost couldn't get enough air. Soon she felt as if she wasn't in complete control of herself because it felt so good that she couldn't have stopped moving if she tried.

On her next stroke, Nick shifted beneath her, and all at once he was inside her. She froze for a moment with a silent gasp, ducking her head and squeezing her eyes closed as the pleasure seemed to go bone-deep. Nick groaned and clamped his hands down on her hips and urged her to move again, faster this time. Then he eased his one hand inward until his palm rested along the crease of her upper thigh, and as she drove down hard on him, he pressed his thumb between her legs and teased her rhythmically. She'd never felt anything like this before. Never. Her heart was thudding and her mind was dizzy with anticipation because she was close…so close…so damned *close*…

Then a barrage of heat and pressure slammed into her,

rocking her wildly, hitting her with one shuddering spasm after another. She threw her head forward, then back, the sheer force of her climax making her body move almost involuntarily, and she had to grit her teeth to muffle the scream of satisfaction that clogged her throat. She couldn't believe it. She couldn't believe what an intense, incredible, glorious sensation it was, and even as the feeling subsided, still she moved against him in a limp, sex-induced haze. Finally, Nick rolled from beneath her and turned her over on her back. Still feeling the aftershocks, she pulled him down on top of her, instinctively reaching between them and guiding him inside her. And astonishingly, within his first few thrusts, she felt a second climax building, and she gasped at the unexpected force of it.

"I'm coming again," she said out loud. "I can't believe—"

"Quiet, sweetheart, quiet—"

"I can't. Nick…oh, *Nick*—"

He clamped his mouth down on hers, stealing her words away, kissing her hard and deep until his breath was her breath but there was barely a breath left between them. When the second climax struck her, she dug her fingertips into his back and arched against him, moaning into his mouth. In that instant, his muscles tightened beneath her hands. His body shuddered above her, a deep, raspy groan rising from his throat. He ripped his mouth from hers and buried his face in the hollow of her neck, his breath coming in short, hard gasps as he continued to move inside her, dragging every bit of pleasure out of the moment that he possibly could.

Finally he slowed, then stopped, but still he was inside her, holding her tightly, his body warm and heavy against hers. Nick paused to swallow hard, then gasped for another breath, and it was a minute before he finally rolled away and took her in his arms. He kissed her and she curled against him, and they lay together, totally spent and totally satisfied.

"Gotta tell you," Nick whispered, "I used to have a lot of dreams about women in this bed. Never thought they'd come true like this."

Sara laughed softly, loving the way his voice sounded in the aftermath of lovemaking, all gruff and breathless, and she promised herself that she wasn't going to think about how after tonight she'd never hear it again. Instead, she simply lay quietly with him until they regained some of their strength, then turned and gave him a hopeful look.

"Again?"

He smiled. "Sara? Are you trying to wear me out?"

"One night. I just want to make the most of it."

He rose on one elbow and stared down at her, his blue eyes shimmering in the dim lamplight. He brushed a strand of hair away from her cheek and kissed her softly.

"Just tell me what you want, sweetheart. I'm all yours."

14

NICK AND SARA left Colorado Springs at noon the next day to drive back to Boulder, and Nick had never felt so miserable in his life. Every mile that sped away beneath them represented one more minute passing before they'd be saying goodbye, and he hated the thought of that.

But it could end no other way.

Still, as they entered Boulder and neared Sara's apartment, the flood of emotion he felt was driving him crazy. Sleeping with her last night had been the most stupid move imaginable, and her leaving him at dawn had just about killed him. Now that he knew what it felt like to make love to her, he'd be torturing himself with thoughts of what he couldn't have from now on.

A few minutes later, he pulled into a parking place near Sara's apartment and killed the engine. Slowly he turned to face her. Bright sunlight streamed through the car window, making her hair shimmer and her skin glow, and he practically had to sit on his hands to keep from reaching for her.

"You've been quiet," he said.

"I was just thinking." She paused. "About last night."

"I hope you don't feel as if I pushed you into it. I just…I just wanted to be with you last night. That's all I can say."

"If you'll remember, I was the one who came to your room."

He smiled. "Oh, yeah."

A long silence stretched between them.

"Look, Sara. I know we said we'd walk away today, but—"

"No. Please don't say it."

"But—"

"I can't risk it. If we kept this up and people found out that something was going on between us, I'd have no credibility left at all. My career is important to me. I can't jeopardize it."

Nick gave her a reluctant nod.

"But it was a wonderful Christmas," she said. "Maybe... maybe the best I've ever had."

She looked away. He saw her blink quickly, as if fighting tears, but when she turned back she gave him a bright smile. "Well. Good luck with the syndication deal."

"And good luck with your new book."

"Well, I'm afraid you messed me up a little with that. As a woman who gave in to you, I can't exactly quote you and then refute you, can I?"

"Do you regret what happened between us?"

"No," she said. "I don't."

"It's our secret. No one will ever know. You trust me on that, don't you?"

"Yes. Of course I do."

They stared at each other a long time, the air quivering between them, the silence pounding in Nick's ears. Finally he just couldn't stop himself. He leaned in to kiss her.

She turned away. "The holiday's over," she said, her voice tight with emotion. "We swore we'd stop."

He nodded, letting out a heavy sigh of resignation. They got out of the car. He grabbed Sara's bag out of the back and handed it to her.

"I'm going to be watching you," Nick said. "I know you're going to have all kinds of success."

"You, too. I might have to tune in to your show every once in a while just to see how you're doing."

"Just do me a favor and always read between the lines, will you?"

She smiled. "Yes. Always."

"Well," he said, glancing around, "it wouldn't do for us to be seen together, so I guess I'd better be going."

"Goodbye, Nick."

"Goodbye, Sara."

They backed away from each other, one step, two. Nick turned and got back into his car, watching as Sara went to her door, unlocked it and slipped inside. She glanced back at him one last time, then shut the door.

And just like that, it was over.

Nick closed his eyes and leaned his head back against the headrest, knowing it was the right thing to do. The only thing to do.

So why did it feel so damned wrong?

SARA WENT inside her apartment, tossed her purse and her bag on the floor beside the front door. She took off her coat, then collapsed on the sofa, feeling as if she were going to cry.

She'd never felt this way about a man before. Never. The ride home had been hell, sitting in that seat next to Nick and wanting him with a desperation that bordered on obsession. And that was a very dangerous thing, because it meant she was running on emotion instead of logic, and she knew from experience just how quickly that got women into all kinds of trouble.

Rationally, she knew what was going on here. Nick was

fun and exciting and the sex had been great, so of course she hated to give that up. But in the end, there were far more important things in life than great sex.

Yes. There were.

Weren't there?

She dropped her head to her hands. Good Lord. If she wasn't even sure of the answer to that question, she really had gone off the deep end. She had to get a grip. Think about her career. Her clients. Her readers.

But no matter how she tried to focus on those things, she kept seeing Nick's face in her mind. She remembered how his hands had felt on her, moving with such shocking sensuality that she hadn't been able to breathe. She heard his voice in the dark, whispering in her ear, making her crazy with wanting him. He was a man who wasn't at all like his reputation, who was good and kind and compassionate and made her feel wonderful in every way.

She sat up on the edge of the sofa. Her stomach felt queasy. Her hands shaky. God, what *was* this?

You can't give him up. You can't.

That thought filled her mind and refused to go away, growing stronger with every breath she took. For the first time in her life, emotions were bombarding her from all sides, obliterating every bit of rational thought she had. She wanted to forget tomorrow and live for today, to be with the one man who made her feel alive in a way she never had before. All the dangers vanished from her mind until all she could see was Nick.

Maybe he hadn't left yet.

Driven by sheer emotion, she leaped to her feet, ran to her front door and yanked it open.

Nick was standing on her front porch.

She froze, staring at him with surprise. He held up his

palm. "Sara. Please. Just listen to me. I know we said we couldn't see each other anymore. I know this is a problem. But I couldn't leave. I know it's all wrong, but I just couldn't—"

She grabbed the sleeve of his coat and yanked him into her apartment. Taking him by the collar, she dragged his lips right down to hers and kissed him. Nick instantly wrapped his arms around her and hauled her up next to him, kicking the door shut with the heel of his boot and kissing her as if it had been years rather than minutes since he saw her last. He backed away for a second, peeled off his coat and let it fall in a heap behind him, and then she curled her hands around his neck and pulled him down to kiss him again.

They started toward her bedroom, unbuttoning clothes with shaking hands, then kissing, then unbuttoning some more. Halfway there, Nick backed Sara against a wall and shoved up her shirt. He unhooked her bra, pushed it aside and kissed her breasts, his hands clutching her waist and holding her in place even as she writhed against him. Lost in the feeling, Sara dropped her head back against the wall, stroking her fingers through his hair, and when he closed his mouth over her nipples and flicked them with his tongue, she thought she'd die from the pleasure of it. She tightened her fingers against his scalp, wishing he'd do this forever at the same time, she wanted *more*.

Finally, she wrenched herself away, grabbed his hand and dragged him into her bedroom, where she climbed onto the bed. She yanked off her shirt and bra, then spun around and fell to her back. As Nick ripped off his clothes, she pulled off her shoes, and by the time she had her pants unzipped he was already there, grabbing them and pulling them off. He crawled up on the bed and hovered over her, staring down at her with a hot, hungry expression that said he wanted her *now.*

"We still have a problem," he said, breathing hard.

"I know."

"A big one. I don't know how we're going to work this out."

"You're here right now. That's all I care about."

He fell to one elbow beside her, curled his hand around her waist and trailed kisses along the column of her neck, sucking and pulling at the tender flesh with his lips, sending warm shivers down her spine.

"Then again," Sara said, tipping her head back as he kissed his way to the hollow of her throat, "if you think about it, the holiday really isn't over."

"How's that?"

"See…it actually runs—" *ahh, what this man could do with his lips* "—from Christmas to New Year's."

Nick ran his hand along her abdomen, then slipped it beneath her panties.

"Which means," she said, her eyes falling closed, "that it's still…a holiday…"

"Yes," he said, sliding his fingers deep inside her, then pulled back to rub in tiny circles. "I hadn't thought of it that way."

Sara couldn't believe how wet she was already, how ready she was for him to make love to her right *now.* She could barely breathe, barely think when he was touching her like this.

"My office is closed this week," she said. "Are you working?"

"No. They're running 'best of' shows."

"Any other plans?"

"A singles meet and greet at Charlie's Bar and Grille

Thursday evening sponsored by the station. I have to toss out a few T-shirts and sign a few boobs."

She froze. "What did you say?"

"Never mind. You don't want to know."

He rolled and pulled her on top of him, and she stretched her body over his. His hands roamed impatiently down her back to grasp the lower curve of her ass. He squeezed firmly, then pulled her tightly against him, his hardness meeting her softness in exactly the right place.

"And I have to put in an appearance at a New Year's Eve party given by the station," Nick said. "But that's it."

Sara dropped a palm to either side of his shoulders and shimmied against him, brushing her nipples across the hard muscles of his chest, almost crying with joy because it felt so good to be with him like this.

"So what we've decided," Nick said, cupping her breasts, lifting and kneading them, "is that it's still a holiday for both of us?" He tweaked and tugged her nipples, and she moaned softly.

"Yes," she said. "Until New Year's Day. If we stay in my apartment, no one will know."

"That's right."

"But then that's it. That's when we'll walk away."

"Yes."

"If anybody finds out—"

"They won't. I swear to you, Sara. They won't."

She crawled to the edge of the bed, yanked her nightstand drawer open and fumbled for a condom. In seconds, he'd rolled it on, and she'd taken off her panties and tossed them aside. He moved between her legs and stared down at her, breathing hard, his blue eyes glazed with passion.

"This is a bad idea, isn't it?" he said.

"Yes, but we're not going to let that stop us, are we?"

"Hell, no."

He plunged inside her, and the surge of sheer pleasure she felt was almost incapacitating. She wrapped her legs around him and pulled him in deep. Within a few strokes, she was already on the verge of coming. She knew why—because lovemaking wasn't just physical with Nick. It was his impatience, his eagerness, his obsession to be with her, and just the madness with which he wanted her could have pushed her over the edge all by itself. She surged against him, rising to meet every thrust, but soon he was moving so hard and so fast that she couldn't keep up and finally she just clutched his shoulders, let him go and let it happen.

And it was happening *now*.

All at once the built-up tension inside her exploded in a burst of energy, wild pulsations rocking her body like a storm tide crashing against a ship. She said his name—no, *screamed* his name—and seconds later, he tensed, groaned, then sank deep inside her in a shuddering climax of his own.

As the sensations wound down, he slowed, stopped, then fell against her, burying his face in the hollow of her neck, his warm breath saturating her skin. Sara rubbed up and down his sweat-sheened back before kissing his shoulder, amazed that she could actually feel his heart beating where his chest was pressed against hers.

Finally, he fell to the bed beside her and took her in his arms. She rested her head on his shoulder and looked up at him.

"That was incredible," she said.

He smiled. "Think the neighbors heard you?"

"They're out of town, thank God."

"Never took you for a screamer. That could have been dangerous at my parents' house."

"Okay, now I'm embarrassed."

"Don't be. I *love* it."

She knew he was serious. He did love it. He loved anything that was outrageous and passionate and just a little bit crazy. And she was growing pretty fond of those things herself.

He blinked lazily, his eyes heavy with satisfaction, then took a deep breath and let it out slowly. "And just think," he said. "We've barely gotten started."

This was a risky thing to do, an experience she wasn't sure she was going to emerge from with her career and her heart intact. But she didn't care. For once in her well-ordered, disciplined, regimented life, she wanted to live for the moment. She wanted to be with Nick, to laugh with him, to make love with him and draw on his electric personality to jumpstart these incredible feelings in her that were so new and fresh and exciting.

One week. Just one.

And she intended to make the most of it.

15

As Nick ran home and packed a bag, Sara made a trip to the grocery store to stock up for the week. The chances of the two of them being recognized together were slim, but still she couldn't risk being seen with him. Since neither of them wanted to get too far from a bed, staying at Sara's apartment was just fine with both of them.

When Nick returned, he parked his car around the corner so no snooping eyes would be able to put the two of them together. And for the next few days, in silent agreement, they didn't talk about the inadvisability of what they were doing or what was going to happen on New Year's Day. Somehow they both knew that if they did, the spell would be broken.

They spent lazy hours lounging in front of the fireplace. They took showers together until they ran out of hot water. They cooked together, ate together, cleaned up together and utilized various foods in alternative ways together. They watched movies. They even played a few games of chess, but it was hard to tell who the best player was, since they had yet to get through a game without getting naked.

And they talked. For endless hours they talked about everything under the sun, and she found that Nick never hesitated to say what was on his mind—to compliment her, to arouse her, to challenge her—and she just couldn't get enough of it.

Fortunately, Karen was out of town for the holiday week so Sara didn't have any explanations to make there. Nick said he had to tell his friend Ted where he was since they saw each other almost every day, but that he could be sworn to silence. Two days after Christmas, Sara's mother called to say she was staying in St. Louis, at least until New Year's. Sara felt that familiar heartache she always did when she knew her mother was making another mistake, but talking to Nick about it helped her put it in perspective.

About the only interruptions they had were occasional calls on Nick's cell phone from his agent, updating him on the progress of the negotiations with Mercury Media. Otherwise, it was just the two of them, reveling in each other.

A few days later, Sara was in the kitchen cleaning up some sugar she'd spilled on the counter, when she looked over to see Nick leaning against the doorway, watching her. His arms were folded across his chest, and he wore nothing but a pair of jeans and a smile. Early on, she'd expressed her preference for that particular look, and he'd expressed his own preference by suggesting that she wear nothing but the shirt he wasn't wearing. She knew that in the future when she thought back to this week, one of the things she would always remember was the feel of his crisp cotton shirts brushing against her thighs and the way he looked at her when she wore them.

He nodded down at the wet rag she held. "Problem?"

"I was aiming for my coffee cup," she said, swiping the rag over the counter. "I missed."

"You're the only person I know who drinks caffeinated coffee after dinner."

"You want me falling asleep early?"

He slipped up behind her, wrapped his arms around her

and kissed her neck. "You don't need coffee, sweetheart. I promise I'll keep you awake."

She turned in his arms and slid her hands around his neck. "So are you getting cabin fever yet?"

"Not in the slightest."

"Still, it can't hurt for you to get out for a little while tonight, right?"

"Wrong." He glanced at his watch, then blew out a breath. "Damn it. I've got to leave pretty soon. But I don't have to stay long. Just mingle with the singles, have a beer, chat a little and head out."

"Wait a minute. I seem to have this memory of you saying something about...signing boobs? What's that all about?"

Nick rolled his eyes. "Do we have to talk about that?"

She smiled. "Oh, yeah. I'm just dying to hear this."

"Well, about a year ago, I was signing publicity photos at some events, and some woman lowered her tank top a little and asked me to sign her breast."

"You've got to be kidding."

"Trust me, Sara. I don't have to make these things up."

"And of course you obliged the lady."

He shrugged. "I thought it was kind of funny at the time. But word got out and now the women love it. I can't get them to stop."

"So you want them to stop?"

"Sometimes I feel like a gynecologist. If you've seen one boob, you've seen them all." He smiled. "Present company excluded, of course."

"Come on, Nick. Signing boobs? Most men would kill to be in your shoes."

"You're right. They would." He caressed her cheek.

"Particularly right now." He gave her a long, delicious kiss that promised even better things when he got home that night.

TWO HOURS LATER, Nick left Charlie's, walking with Ted through lightly falling snow, trying to remember a time when loud music, singles on the prowl and excessive alcohol consumption had been a recipe for a fun evening. Actually, he might have been able to work up at least a little enthusiasm about it if only he hadn't had something so much better to compare it to.

Such as going home to Sara.

"So how many women gave you their phone numbers tonight?" Ted asked.

Nick dug a few wadded up cocktail napkins out of his pocket and slapped them into Ted's palm.

"Okay," Ted said, "let's see what we've got here. This one is from April. She was the little blonde, right? She dots her *i* with a heart. How sweet." He turned to Nick. "Aren't they supposed to card sixteen-year-olds at the door?"

"She said she was twenty-two."

"No way. She was jailbait." He dropped the napkin and looked at the next one. "Danielle? Wasn't she the one with all the eye makeup who was still wearing a wedding ring?"

"Uh-huh."

Ted dropped that one, too, and read the next one. "Ah. Now you're cooking. This one's from Brandi. I saw you sign her boob. You could have written the entire Declaration of Independence across that one."

Ted handed the napkin to Nick, but Nick held up his palm. "Keep it. She's all yours."

"Hmm. I'm guessing you have another woman on your mind. How are things going with Sara?"

"Picture the best time you've ever had with a woman."

"Yeah?"

"Now multiply that by ten."

Ted eyed him carefully. "So it's going to be just one week? Are you sure about that?"

Nick tried to picture that goodbye. Even though he knew it had to come, still he just couldn't fathom it.

"Anything more is too risky for Sara," he said. "If people find out she's messing around with me, how is she in any position to tell women to stay away from men like me? Her whole career is built on that."

"Good point. But Sara's not the only one who's at risk."

"What do you mean?"

"Come on, Nick. Haven't you thought about what this could mean for you, too?"

"What are you talking about?"

They stopped at Ted's car. "Okay. Suppose your fans got wind of the fact that you're suddenly getting serious about a sharp, mature, conservative woman like Sara. Talk about a reputation killer. The guys love you because you're living their dream life—the man about town with a different woman in his bed every night. The women love you because they picture themselves being one of those women."

"So if I get serious about Sara—"

"You're no longer the Nick Chandler they know and love."

Nick hadn't really considered that he could get burned by this, too. After all, the only way it could cause a problem for him was if he and Sara had an ongoing relationship. That wasn't going to happen, so what was there to worry about?

"It's really not like that," Nick said. "I'm not getting serious about her."

"The world is full of women, but syndication deals don't come along every day. Don't screw it up."

"Don't worry, Ted. You know how much I want this. I'm not going to screw it up."

"I've never seen you make an idiot of yourself over a woman before. Don't start now."

"I'm not going to."

"I know where you end up in this business if you don't go big. You want to end up producing a gardening show? If I can't be an inspiration to you, at least let me be a warning."

"Will you stop ranting? I hear you."

"You will be at the New Year's Eve party, won't you?"

"Of course I will," Nick said. "Mitzi has commanded it."

"She's right. You need to meet the big dude and hammer the deal home."

Nick nodded. No matter how much he deplored the idea of a formal party, he knew face time with Mr. Big could be critical to closing the deal, and he fully intended to be there.

He said goodbye to Ted, then headed for Sara's apartment. Nick didn't know why his friend was so worried, because he had this thing in perspective. He and Sara had been upfront with each other. They knew whatever was happening between them would be coming to a halt on New Year's Day. It would be fun while it lasted, but when it was over, it was over.

Using the key Sara had given him, he unlocked her door and went inside, surprised to find the house nearly dark. He hung up his coat, then went around the corner into the living room.

All the lamps were turned off, and the only light in the room came from the glow of the fireplace. Sara sat on a blanket in front of it, leaning comfortably against the hearth, her knees pulled up to her chest. She wore nothing but one of his shirts, the sleeves rolled to her forearms, the tail grazing her thighs. The glow of the firelight bathed one side of her face, leaving the other side in darkness, and her hair fell over her shoulders like golden rainwater. She looked beautiful. Intriguing. Sexy. Captivating.

And all that perspective he supposedly had went straight to hell.

"How was it?" she asked.

"Just another day at the office."

"Come here."

The low, enticing sound of those two tiny words had him aroused already. He walked over to the edge of the blanket, and she stared up at him, her green eyes glittering in the firelight.

"Take off your clothes."

16

NICK'S HEART jolted, but he managed a lazy smile. "Now, sweetheart, if I take off my clothes, then I'll be naked, and you'll still have clothes on. That's not quite fair, is it?"

"I've decided that fair play is overrated."

Okay. No problem. If she wanted him naked, who was he to argue? Given the fact that she'd tossed three or four condoms onto the blanket beside her, she clearly intended to get naked herself sooner or later. He could be patient.

For a little while anyway.

He slowly unbuttoned his cuffs, then the front of his shirt, and took it off. When he pulled off everything south of his waist, he was surprised at how unabashedly she stared at him, as if his only purpose in life right now was to entertain her.

And he had no problem with that, either.

Her gaze slowly played down his body and back up again, her chest rising and falling with a deep intake of breath. "You're one gorgeous man, Nick. Did I ever tell you that?"

"Not in so many words. But please. Flatter me."

"As if you need the ego boost."

"I just like hearing you say it."

She tossed a sofa pillow onto the blanket. "Lie down."

He sat down next to her and leaned in to kiss her. She put her fingertips against his lips.

"Nick, I believe I said to lie down."

He had no idea what she was up to, but he didn't mind playing along to find out. For a moment, he actually felt a little self-conscious lying there naked while she was still relatively clothed; the raging hard-on he already had was only making matters worse. But when Sara said strip, he wasn't about to say no.

He reached for her shirt buttons, but she caught his hand and gave him a look of admonishment.

"Sorry, Nick. New rule."

"So now you're making rules?"

"Who do you think I learned that from?"

He gave her a sheepish look. "Oh, yeah."

"I want you to put your hands under the pillow, right beneath your head. Both of them."

He blinked with surprise. "Why?"

"Because I'm dying to do the most incredible things to your body, but it looks as if your hands are going to keep getting in the way."

The images her words stirred up sent a jolt of electricity straight to his groin. If he was hard before, he was the Rock of Gibraltar now.

"If you're trying to turn me on, it's working," he said, sliding his hands beneath the pillow. "Though I gotta say that I never thought of you as the kinky type."

"Nothing kinky about it. It's the only way I know of to make sure you behave yourself."

"Okay, Sara. You've got five minutes. Then you're getting naked."

She leaned in and whispered in his ear. "Don't mess with me, Nick. I'll take all night if I want to. Or, more to the point…" She touched her tongue to a spot just beneath his ear, then kissed it softly. "If *you* want me to."

Nick couldn't believe the way just those few whispered words made him feel—all hot and bothered and thrilled that she was enjoying herself, because there had been a time when he'd wondered if she would ever let go like this. The past few days had brought surprises he'd never anticipated, and he couldn't even imagine what tomorrow would reveal.

Sara leaned away, her legs tucked to one side, resting one palm on the blanket. Her gaze traveled down his body, stopping here and there to focus for a moment before moving on again.

"Sara?"

"Shh. I'm thinking."

"About what?"

"You'll find out soon enough." A sly smile stole across her lips. "Maybe you'd better close your eyes."

He let his eyes drift closed. For a long time, all he sensed was the crackling of the fire and its warmth filling the room and the faint scent of Sara's perfume. Since he had no idea what she had in mind, his whole body felt hypersensitive, waiting for her touch.

After what seemed like an eternity, her lips brushed his chest. Just her lips, not her hands, and it startled him enough that he flinched.

"You're so jumpy, Nick," she said, her hot breath spilling over his skin. "You need to relax."

"Relax? You're joking, right?"

She dropped more featherlight kisses against his chest, then worked her way slowly down to his abdomen, touching him with her lips only. When she came within millimeters of his penis, he held his breath, closing his hands into fists underneath the pillow, waiting until he finally felt her lips again…

On his upper thigh.

She touched her tongue to the place she'd kissed, moving it in tiny circles, almost tickling but not quite, then easing over to his other thigh and doing the same thing. Just that tiny touch was making him absolutely crazy.

Five minutes? Who the hell had he been kidding? Big talk for a man who wasn't going to last thirty seconds at this rate, and she hadn't even touched him *there* yet.

Sara kissed her way from his thigh to his knee and all the way down his shin, occasionally dragging her lips across him or teasing him with her tongue. Then she worked her way back up, and when she reached his thigh again, anticipation surged through him when he thought about where she might be going next. She kissed the hollow just inside his hip bone, a spot so sensitive that he dug his fingernails into the pillow, sure he was going to have to apologize later for ripping it to shreds. She gave him one kiss after another, moving closer… closer…

Then he felt the oddest sensation.

He opened his eyes, and what he saw almost made him come on the spot. Sara was on her knees, her palms on the floor, backlit by the fire, and he could see the outline of her naked body beneath his shirt. She was hovering over his penis, huffing her warm breath right over the tip. Just the sight of her mouth so close to him and her hair draped across her cheek and shining in the firelight excited the hell out of him. He squeezed his eyes closed again, his breath coming faster, every muscle tense, desperate for her to take him in her mouth, desperate to feel her lips on him again. And then he did.

On his chest.

He went limp against the blanket, groaning softly, wondering if he'd ever been this hard in his life without doing something about it. Wondering if he'd ever been this hard in his life, *period.*

"Sara…" he said, his voice choked, "you're making me crazy here…"

She didn't respond. Instead, she eased up to his neck, where she wet her lips and placed a moist, heavy kiss right beneath his ear. The hot shivers that emanated from that tiny spot radiated through his whole body. He clenched his hands beneath the pillow, about two seconds away from grabbing her, tossing her down on the blanket and having his way with her. But he remained still even as he clawed the pillow beneath his head, letting her tease her tongue against his earlobe, then drag her lips along his cheek to plant a warm, lush kiss right on his mouth.

"Nick?"

"Yes?"

"I've kissed you just about everywhere I can think of. Do you know of anyplace I missed?"

His eyes sprang open. "Anyplace you missed? Are you kidding me?"

She took a slow visual tour down his body again, then gave him an innocent shrug.

"Okay! That's it!" He yanked his hands from beneath the pillow and sat up, giving her a no-nonsense look. "You. Naked. Now."

She placed her palm against her chest, blinking innocently. "Why, Nick. Is something the matter?"

"Sara, if you don't take that shirt off, I'm ripping it off."

She glanced down. "Well, it is your shirt. I suppose if you want to tear it up…"

"Sara!"

Barely hiding her smug smile, she unfastened two buttons and pulled the shirt off over her head. Nick caught it halfway up, yanked it off the rest of the way, then slung it on the floor. In seconds he had one of the condoms on, and didn't even bother to pull her panties off. He just moved between her legs and shoved the silky fabric aside.

"Wait a minute," Sara said. "What about my panties? I thought you wanted me to be—"

He plunged inside her, and she threw her head back with a moan of pleasure.

"—naked."

She let out a long breath of satisfaction, curling her legs around his hips and pulling him deep inside. "Never mind. I'm naked enough. Just don't stop doing this."

He eased back until he'd pulled out almost all the way, amazed that just kissing him had made her so hot that he moved inside her with no resistance at all. He smiled to himself. The fact that she was so ready for him was going to make what he was about to do next even more fun.

On his next thrust, she clutched his biceps and arched her hips up to meet him, but he paused just long enough that she'd settled back down to the blanket by the time he entered her. He slid out, then back in several more times. She rocked her hips up to meet him, but with a little careful timing he kept her out of sync.

"Nick," she said, breathing hard, "this is very nice, but—"

"But what?"

She growled in frustration. "Come on, Nick! I'm pretty darned sure you know how to do this. I've experienced it firsthand, you know. So would you please—"

"You were a very bad girl, Sara."

He moved deep inside her again, but so slowly that she gritted her teeth with frustration.

"What...what do you mean?"

"You were having such fun teasing me, weren't you?"

"No! I wasn't teasing you. I was just..."

"Just what?"

She went limp beneath him. "Oh, boy," she muttered. "This is payback, isn't it?"

"You think?"

He pulled back, then entered her again. And again. And again. *Very* slowly. He was dying to move faster, but he made sure that no matter how hard she dug her fingers into his shoulders and how desperately she shimmied beneath him, all she got for her effort was a heaping dose of sexual frustration.

"Okay," she said, breathing hard. "I was a bad girl. I admit it. I was teasing you. It was an awful, rotten thing to do, and I should be ashamed of myself." She took his face in her hands, lifted her shoulders off the blanket and kissed him. "Just make love to me. Right now. *Please.*"

"Only if you promise to do it again."

"Huh?"

"Did I say I didn't like it?"

Sara groaned and thunked her head back against the blanket. Then she rose again, slid her arms around his neck and kissed him hard on the lips. "I'm all yours, Nick. I'll do anything you want me to as long as it's somewhat moral and marginally legal."

"You mean next time around you might actually find that last place to kiss?"

"It'll be the *first* place I kiss. But right now, would you *please*—"

He did. But harder this time, and faster, and soon all the

teasing went away and he was holding her tightly and they were moving together in perfect rhythm. She curled her arms around his neck and clamped her thighs around him, and he thrust inside her over and over and over, driving himself into a frenzy of sensation, familiar enough with her body by now to know he was doing the same to her.

The tightness and the pressure and the unbelievable heat of her made everything inside him feel like molten rock, and when she began to shudder beneath him and call out his name, that was all it took to send him over the edge, too. He let out a fierce groan as pulse after pulse of red-hot electricity shot through him, making him quiver with the sheer force of it.

When the feeling finally subsided, he dropped his forehead against Sara's shoulder, trying to catch his breath, unable to believe how every time he made love with her it was better than the last. Still gasping for air, he rolled to one side and just lay there, sprawled out on the blanket, every muscle limp and spent. With great effort, Sara rose on one elbow and started to say something, only to fall back to the blanket again just as exhausted as he was.

"God, Nick," she said, swallowing hard between gasping breaths. "We're gonna kill each other."

He rolled his head around to look at her. "Yeah, but what a way to go."

When she smiled at him, he felt a surge of contentment, the kind that came with knowing how much he pleased her, how much she enjoyed being with him like this. He could tell that up to now sex had always been a serious experience for her, and now that she'd found the fun in it, she couldn't get enough of it.

Enough of him.

The woman he'd met that first day at the station would

never have behaved the way she had tonight. He loved how she'd turned from an uptight woman afraid to let herself go to a sassy, sexy woman who teased him and laughed with him until they were making love with the eagerness of a pair of teenagers fogging up car windows.

Sara was so much more than he'd ever expected her to be. Being with her was like winning the lottery, or unwrapping a particularly gorgeous present, only to find the gift inside was ten times better than the wrapping.

Keep this in perspective. On New Year's Day, it's over.

He sighed. Perspective. Right. Who the hell had he been kidding?

He pulled Sara into his arms, already thinking about what crazy thing he could do with her next time to amuse her or creatively frustrate her or simply turn her on more than she'd ever been turned on in her life, when suddenly there was a knock at her door.

17

SARA'S HEART jumped at the sudden noise. She sat up quickly, then rose and walked to the door. She looked out the peephole, then turned back to Nick and whispered, "It's Heather."

"Your assistant? What's she doing here?"

"I don't know, but I need to answer the door. I'll go get a robe. Can you get that stuff out of the living room?"

As Sara ran to her bedroom, Nick grabbed their clothes along with the blanket. As she was coming out of her bedroom, she met him going in. She gave him a quick kiss. "I just need to find out what she wants. I'll be back soon."

She threw on the robe, flipped on lights in the living room, then went to the door. When she opened it, Heather stared back at her, her eyes bloodshot and her face tearstained.

"Heather?"

"I'm sorry, Sara. I shouldn't be bothering you at home like this. But after what happened—"

When she put her hand over her mouth and started to cry again, Sara pulled her inside and took her to sit on the sofa.

"Tell me what's wrong," she said.

Heather heaved a huge, shaky sigh. "Well...you know I broke up with Richard, right?"

"Yes?"

"And I felt so good about that. It hurt a lot, but still I felt good that I'd finally done it. Then…then he called me this afternoon."

Oh, boy. Sara knew what was coming now. "What did he say?"

"He told me he missed me so much, and that he knew he'd treated me badly and he wanted to make up for it. He wanted to come to my apartment tonight. He sounded so sincere that I told him I missed him, too, and that he could come over."

This was always the point at which, for all her training, Sara simply wanted to shake some sense into women. Didn't they see how easily they were being manipulated?

"But then tonight came," Heather said, "and he didn't show up. I waited an hour. Then two hours. And I tried to call him, but he didn't answer. He didn't answer his cell phone, either. And then I got worried. You know, that something might have happened to him. So…" She exhaled. "God, I feel so *dumb*."

"Go ahead. Tell me what happened."

"I went over to his apartment. Just to check on him, you know? To make sure he was okay. But when I knocked, another…" Her voice choked up. "Another woman answered the door."

Sara sighed. "Oh, Heather…"

"And then Richard was there, standing behind her, just looking at me as if he hadn't even called me, as if I didn't mean anything to him. I could see he and this woman had been…"

Heather put her hand over her mouth to stifle another sob. "I—I just turned around and ran. And then I came here. I'm sorry." She sniffed, then wiped her eyes. "I just felt so bad, and I didn't know what else to do…"

"I'm glad you came to see me. You did the right thing."

Sara took her hand and started talking to her, wishing she could wave that proverbial magic wand that would instill a little self-esteem into women like Heather so things like this would never happen again.

But there was no magic solution to a problem like this.

They talked for the next hour, and Sara hoped that maybe this time the things she said to Heather would stick, that the next time she was faced with this kind of situation she'd make the right decision and tell Richard to go to hell. But still, Sara knew how unlikely that was. Even if Richard left the picture, sooner or later some other guy would come along and treat her badly and the whole cycle would start all over again.

Sometimes it felt so futile. In spite of her counsel, women like Heather continued to make the same mistakes, and Sara wondered sometimes just how much good she was actually doing.

FOR THE PAST HOUR, Nick had lain on Sara's bed, able to hear just enough of her conversation with Heather to get the gist of what was going on. When he finally heard the front door open and close, he met Sara back in the living room.

"I overheard you and Heather talking," he said. "Hope you don't mind."

"No. It's okay."

"How is she?"

"Better now. But I'm not so sure I am."

"What's the matter?"

"To tell you the truth, Nick, what I do drives me crazy sometimes."

He put his arm around her and led her to the sofa. "Okay, doctor," he said as they sat down, "tell me all about it."

"They just seem to keep doing it. Again and again. No

matter what I say, still they make the same mistakes." She shrugged weakly. "I guess that's what's bothering me."

"That, and the fact that you see your mother in girls like her?"

She sighed. "You're being insightful again, Nick. Didn't I tell you to knock that off?"

"It's true, isn't it?"

She leaned into him, and he put his arm around her. "Yeah. It's true. I can't help thinking that it's always possible that a woman like Heather will end up pregnant. And if she's still making those bad decisions, then suddenly some poor kid is subjected to her emotional roller coaster. I lived that life, and I don't want anyone else to have to go through it."

"I don't understand why women don't just tell guys like him to go to hell."

"Because those guys are deceptive. When they're nice, they're very, very nice. But when they're bad..."

"But shouldn't that be obvious?" Nick said. "Shouldn't women be able to see when they're being jerked around? Why do they put up with it?"

"You said it yourself that day when you interviewed me. Some women like men who are just a little bit dangerous."

Nick blinked with surprise. "But I didn't mean dangerous as in hurtful. I meant dangerous as in fun and exciting and..."

He stopped short. For the first time, he heard the meaning of that word from Sara's point of view, and it shocked him.

"Heather said that Richard listens to your show all the time."

Nick felt a twinge of defensiveness. "Do you think I tell men to treat women like that?"

"No. Of course not. Not directly." She paused. "But when you interview a man who brags about sleeping with a thousand women—"

"I play that kind of guest for laughs. Nothing else. I never try to justify what he's doing."

"But the message is still there. You're telling your listeners that sex is nothing more than cheap recreation. That it's quantity that counts, not quality. Most people are going to get the humor in that kind of guest and ignore the rest. But some aren't."

"My show is pure entertainment. That's all. If a guy treats his girlfriend badly, that's his fault, not mine."

"I'm not accusing you of anything, Nick. I'm just saying that you may have more influence than you think. Young men listen to your show, and undoubtedly they'd love to be just like you."

Nick remembered what Ted had said. *The guys love you because you're living their dream life—the man about town with a different woman in his bed every night.*

He'd goofed around with guys like Richard on the air for years now, and if the syndication deal came through, he'd be doing it for many more. Of course, those guys weren't all bad. But how many of them took the things he said and twisted them into their own brand of bad behavior? And how many of those guys thought he was just like them?

And why had he never stopped to really consider that?

But the truth was that he couldn't consider it. Not right now. Where his livelihood was concerned, he was on an express train with no way off.

"It's just a radio show," he told Sara. "I'm not going to take the rap for the fact that some guys mistreat women. And I couldn't change what I'm doing even if I wanted to. Not with this syndication deal coming through. Do you have any idea the kind of money I'd be giving up if I stopped being that guy?"

"A lot, I imagine."

"I'm on the brink of my career really taking off. I have no intention of stopping now."

"I know you don't. You told me when we were at your parents' house that you'd do anything to make it happen. I believe you then." She paused. "And I believe you now."

He heard the disapproval in her voice, the inference that he was shooting straight up the ladder, but maybe it was the wrong ladder to climb.

"But even though I have to continue doing what I'm doing," Nick said, "it doesn't mean I'm the person my listeners think I am."

"You're not?"

"Is that the only way you see me? As that guy on the air?"

"We're having a one-week fling, Nick. That's not exactly inconsistent with your reputation."

"But this means one hell of a lot more to me than—"

He stopped short.

"Than what?" she asked.

He wasn't sure. All at once he was looking at his life from a whole new angle. Sara was different than any other woman he'd ever been with, exciting him in ways he'd never felt before at the same time she made him feel steady and grounded. For the first time, the idea of coming home to the same woman every day was intensely appealing, so much so that he hated the prospect of their relationship coming to an end. But how was he supposed to tell her that?

"I'm just not going to like saying goodbye to you," he murmured.

"It's going to be hard for me, too." Sara slid her hand

over his thigh, stroking it gently. "See, Nick, the truth is that I know you're not the man your listeners hear every day on the air. Oh, some of it is you and always will be. The humor. The irreverence. The sexy commentary about damned near everything." She smiled briefly, then grew solemn again. "But I've also seen the kindness. The compassion. The determination to give a certain woman a holiday season she'll never forget." She lay her head on his shoulder. "I just wish the man I've gotten to know was the man you could show everyone else."

Suddenly Nick felt as if he were hemmed in with no way out, and the pressure was stifling. The syndication people, his producer, his agent—all of them wanted him to be even more of that man Sara didn't like.

The man he wasn't even sure he liked himself.

Sara was right. He *was* two different people. There had been a time when he'd been far more like his listeners than he cared to admit, but lately things had changed. Slowly, without him really realizing it, the man he was on air had become more of a character he played than a lifestyle he lived. When he went to events like the one he'd gone to tonight at Charlie's, he stood there talking and laughing and drinking and being exactly who those people expected him to be, but he didn't feel connected to any of it. With Sara, he felt connected.

And the day after tomorrow, she would be gone.

"I wish we hadn't even started talking about this," Nick said. "We don't have much time left. I don't want to spend it disagreeing."

Sara sighed. "I know. I don't either."

"It's just me here right now, Sara. Not that other guy."

She laid her palm against his face and kissed him. "Don't worry. This is the man I'm always going to remember."

Nick took her in his arms, and soon he was drowning her in long, leisurely kisses, trying to imprint her scent, her taste, her touch on his brain for those times in the future when all he would have would be memories. Soon they moved to the bedroom, where he glanced at the clock on the nightstand and saw the LCD readout switch from 10:42 to 10:43.

One more minute gone.

They fell into bed, where their lovemaking was slow and erotic, with a bittersweet edge that came from knowing that tomorrow was New Year's Eve and their time together was almost up.

NICK AND SARA spent the next day together as they had the others, but through it all Sara felt as if there were a clock inside her head, ticking off the minutes, and by the time they sat down to dinner, the sound was deafening. Even though Nick was trying not to let her see him do it, she saw him checking his watch a time or two as they ate.

"Well," she said, as they finished eating, "I think you've put it off as long as you can. It's after seven o'clock."

Nick sighed. "Yeah, I know. If I don't get dressed and get to that party, my agent is going to have a stroke."

"Why don't you go get ready, and I'll clean this up?"

"I've got a better idea. I've got to take a shower—" he leaned in and kissed her "—and I hate to shower alone."

Sara thought back to a few of their shower escapades, and she couldn't say yes fast enough.

A while later, after drying off and finally regaining the use of all her muscle groups, she headed to the kitchen to clean up. After closing the dishwasher and turning it on, she heard Nick come out of her bedroom. She peeked into the living room, and the moment she saw him, she fell back against the doorway, her hand on her chest, her mouth hanging open in astonishment.

Maybe if she'd been in the room as he was dressing, the gradual transformation wouldn't have been as stunning. But getting hit with Nick Chandler in a tuxedo all at once was a mind-blowing experience. The formal clothes gave him an irresistible mix of cool sophistication and roguish charm that was going to make every woman at that party tonight faint dead away.

Nick saw Sara's expression and froze. "What?"

"What do you mean, *what?* You look *incredible*."

He tugged at his shirt collar, rolling his eyes. "Yeah, right. Hand me a martini. Shaken, not stirred."

She walked over to him and ran her hands up his lapels, then circled them around his neck. "Trust me, Nick. There hasn't been a James Bond yet who looks half as good as you do right now."

"Look out, Sara. All this flattery is going to make my ego shoot right off the charts. You wouldn't like me when I'm full of myself."

"Actually, Nick, in spite of my accusations in the past, you're surprisingly nonegotistical. Only one of many things to like about you."

He wrapped his arms around her. "Tell me more."

"No time right now. Check back with me when you have an hour or so to listen."

Nick sighed. "I'm really sorry I have to go. The last thing I want to do is leave you tonight."

"I know."

He brushed her hair away from her face and kissed her. "I can't believe this. For the first time there's a woman I'm dying to kiss at midnight, and she's going to be clear across town."

"You've never kissed a woman at midnight? I find that hard to believe."

"I've had dozens of midnight kisses. And not one of them was special to me in the least. That's why I wish I was going to be with you."

"I never have," Sara said.

"What?"

"Had a kiss at midnight."

"What? You've never had a kiss on New Year's Eve?"

"I'm afraid not."

"Then here's what we'll do. Don't watch Times Square. Tape it. When I get home, we can replay it and pretend it's earlier."

"We'll just use our imaginations?"

"It worked with the mistletoe, didn't it?"

She smiled even though her heart wasn't in it. Right now, she would have liked nothing more than to go back to that Christmas Eve mistletoe and start all over again.

"I'll come home as soon as I can after midnight," Nick said.

"I'll be waiting for you."

He put on his coat, but before he left, she leaned in close and whispered something in his ear that was hot and sexy and just a little bit crazy, something she hoped would make him hurry home as fast as possible.

NICK STEPPED into the marble-tiled lobby of the Brownleigh Hotel and checked his coat, then stood for a moment at the door of the ballroom. It was filled with radio station personnel, local celebrities, KZAP advertisers and the brass from Mercury Media.

Mitzi spotted him and hurried across the room. "Where have you been? It's nearly nine o'clock!"

"It's a New Year's party, Mitzi. It goes until midnight."

"And don't *ever* turn your phone off at such a critical time. How am I supposed to get in touch with you?"

"Lighten up, will you? I'm here now. Just point me to the asses I need to kiss."

A calculating smile spread across her face. "Okay. At least you're on the right wavelength." She nodded toward a table-ful of balding men in tuxes and their sequin-covered wives.

"Okay. Let me give you the lay of the land. The guy about to pop out of his cummerbund is Rayburn, the top dog. That's his wife on his right. Morris, the number two guy, is on his left, with his wife next to him. They've had enough alcohol to loosen them up, and they're definitely here to party. I'll introduce you, and then I want you to show them the Nick Chandler they're buying."

"No problem."

"Deluge them with that scintillating personality of yours."

"I hear you."

"I want you to glow in the dark, Nick. Are you getting me?"

"I got you the first time."

"And be sure to charm the hell out of their wives. I'm betting they have a lot of pull with their husbands."

"That's not a problem, either." Nick took a deep breath. "Let's go."

SARA SAT on her sofa, looking at her watch every five minutes and feeling miserable. Nick was going to be gone for hours. Midnight would come and go, and still she'd be sitting here, waiting for him to come home.

She leaned her head against the back of the sofa, closing her eyes and thinking back to the first time she'd walked into the radio station and laid eyes on him. She never would have guessed that the man she'd gotten to know would fuel her dreams and touch her heart the way he had. Now she was going to have to say goodbye to him, and this time there would be no reprieves.

She thought about how Nick had told her that he'd kissed dozens of girls at midnight. She'd never experienced that. Not once. Just the thought of him taking her in his arms as the ball was dropping in Times Square and then kissing her amid all that cheering sent shivers down her spine.

The more she thought about it, the more obsessed she became with the image, thinking how wonderful it would be to be to start off the new year with somebody who was special to her. To have Nick kiss her breathless, then toast the coming year with a bottle of champagne.

It would be a perfect evening. Absolutely perfect.

Suddenly the most outrageous thought popped into Sara's mind. She sat up straight, thinking about it, then slumped against the sofa again.

No. She couldn't do it. It was already nine o'clock on New Year's Eve. How was she supposed to pull it off?

She thought about it some more, though, and suddenly she was on the edge of her seat again. Would it hurt to make a phone call and check out the possibilities?

She hurried to the kitchen and pulled out a phone book, thinking maybe she could have that midnight kiss after all.

18

NICK SPENT the next hour giving the executives from Mercury Media as much of Nick Chandler as he possibly could. He filled them in on his years in broadcasting that led to the show he was doing now, making himself sound as colorful as he possibly could, which eventually led him to entertain the group with a few stories about some of the outrageous things that had happened in the studio during live broadcasts. At the same time, he flirted with the women just enough that they'd find him charming without their husbands finding him a threat. For a couple of hours, he kept it light, kept them laughing, and after their lengthy conversation, he got the unmistakable feeling that things were moving in the right direction.

Eventually, Rayburn excused himself, along with Morris, and they headed off across the ballroom. Nick headed to the bar. Ted came up beside him, his coat missing in action and his tie dangling around his neck. By all indications, he'd visited the bar one too many times already.

"So how's it going?" he asked Nick.

"So far, so good."

"Those guys look pretty darned happy. I think you're on the right track."

"Let's hope so."

"So…how's Sara?"

Nick had been trying to keep his thoughts off of her tonight and on the matter at hand. He hadn't been succeeding very well, but he'd been trying.

"She's good."

"Is tomorrow still D-Day?"

"Yes, Ted. It is."

And thanks for reminding me of that, too.

A man came up beside Nick. "Nick Chandler?"

"Yes?"

"I'm the manager of the Brownleigh." He handed Nick an envelope. "I was asked to give this to you."

"What is it?"

"I was told it would be self-explanatory." He smiled. "Have a nice evening."

As the man walked away, Ted nodded down at the envelope. "What's that?"

Nick opened it. Inside it was a room key and a note. And the moment he saw it, he rolled his eyes. Good Lord. As if he hadn't seen about a hundred of these over the years?

"Okay," Ted said. "Which woman here wants you to join her for a little after-party rendezvous?"

Nick opened the note. *If you can get away, I'd love that midnight kiss. Room 617. I'll be waiting.*

His heart leaped. This wasn't from one of the women here tonight.

This was from Sara.

He stared at the key, almost laughing out loud at the rush of pure pleasure it gave him. He already knew she was smart, sexy and beautiful. Now he could add another of his favorite characteristics to the list. *Spontaneous.*

"It's from Sara," Nick said. "She's here."

Ted's eyes widened. "Checked in?"

"Yeah."

"You're kidding. Did you know she was going to do that?"

"Nope."

"Man, you were right. She's something else. Are you going up there?"

Nick smiled. "Wouldn't you?"

"I'll have to get back to you on that. You know. The next time a beautiful woman invites me to her hotel room."

"Don't breathe a word of this, Ted. You hear me?"

"Kid, we've been keeping each other's secrets for years. Why stop now?"

Nick checked his watch. It was eleven thirty, and he was completely schmoozed out for the evening. Why did he need to stay until midnight? They probably wouldn't even notice if he left.

"Nick! There you are!"

He turned to see Mitzi approaching, striding along like a diminutive drill sergeant. "I just talked to Rayburn. He wants to see you."

"What for?"

"Not sure, but he's sure acting jovial. That can only be a good thing."

Okay. Not to worry. He still had plenty of time to chat a little more, then get upstairs. He slid the key and the note into his pocket and followed Mitzi back to Rayburn's table.

SARA SAT on the bed in Room 617, wearing a daring black satin gown she'd bought on a whim a few months ago, but never had the nerve to wear. She smiled to herself. Nick was going to love it.

She'd turned out all the lights and tuned the television to the Times Square New Year's celebration. She'd opened the drapes to reveal a nighttime view of city lights, and a bottle of champagne was chilling. A call to the hotel manager verified that her note had been delivered.

Now all she could do was wait.

She'd lucked out with the hotel. They'd had a guest who hadn't shown up, and they'd been more than happy to give her the room at the last minute. She didn't think about the risk she took in coming here. She didn't think about the tomorrows she and Nick weren't going to have. All she thought about was this one night and the kiss she wanted more than anything.

She sneaked a peek at her watch, and her heart sank a little. It was eleven forty.

She knew from the beginning that there was no guarantee that Nick would be able to get away, but she refused to dwell on that. He *would* be coming up here. By the time that ball dropped on Times Square, she'd be in his arms again.

WHEN NICK and Mitzi arrived at Rayburn's table, the men stood up, and Nick could tell they were well-infused with holiday cheer. And those vibes again. They seemed to leap off both men and shoot straight at Nick.

"Morris and I have been talking," Rayburn said, "and now we'd like to talk to you."

"Yes?" Nick said.

"I'll get right to the point. We like your show. We like it a lot. But our opinion doesn't mean crap unless we've got hard data to justify going wide with it. Over the past month, we've been doing a lot of demographic research in a lot of markets, and we've pinpointed a few cities around the country that we think might be able to use a dose of Nick Chandler. Advertisers have shown considerable interest in your show. You've got a narrow appeal, but your

listeners are loyal as hell. We're convinced that will trans-
late to other markets, as well. After all that, there was really only one piece of the puzzle left, and that was the man
himself."

Nick's heart was beating rapid-fire.

"Your agent plays hardball," Rayburn said, glancing at
Mitzi. "She keeps insisting that you're worth every penny
of that outrageous salary she's demanding. But after tonight, I'm inclined to agree. We had no intention of making a decision on the spot, but after talking about it, we see
no reason to postpone it." He held out his hand. "We have
a deal."

Nick was shocked. As he shook Rayburn's hand, excitement surged through him. It had happened. The one thing
he'd worked for years now had finally come to pass, and
he felt so pumped up he could barely speak.

"Twelve stations the first of next month," Rayburn said.
"Then we'll go from there."

"Thank you, Mr. Rayburn," he said. "I'm glad to be on
board."

"Just give your national audience the same stuff you've
been giving your local audience, and you're going straight
to the top."

Straight to the top.

Just those words made chills run up and down Nick's
spine. He had a sudden flash of all the years he'd spent as
a DJ and then as a host of his own show, working hard,
honing the bits he did, playing his guests for all they were
worth, building up his rapport with his listeners.

And it had finally paid off.

What happened next was a blur. Rayburn took him up
on the stage and made the announcement that his show
was moving into syndication, and suddenly Nick was

doing what he did best—talking and joking and saying
brilliant things about Mercury Media like the team player
he intended to be. Somebody stuck a glass of champagne
in his hand and somebody else toasted his success. For
once, he was even glad that Raycine had crashed the party
with her photographer in tow. Tomorrow she'd be telling
all of Boulder that he'd finally hit the big time. A high-pro-
file party topped off by big news like this was just the kind
of stuff he could count on her to spread around.

The whole time he was standing up there, Nick felt as
if he were moving through a dream. He pictured buying
a Lexus, driving down to Colorado Springs and running
it past his brother. Hell, what was he saying? Forget the
Lexus. He'd always had a thing for Jags. He was really
more the sports car type, anyway, and that would make
Brent green with envy.

God, that was going to be fun.

The people from the station gathered around to congrat-
ulate him, and Ted got a little crazy and dumped half a bottle of champagne over Nick's head, but everybody was in
such a party spirit it was no big deal. Because it was near-
ing midnight, more champagne was passed around, until
everyone in the place had a glass. The stars in Nick's eyes
were absolutely blinding. He never could have imagined
that this night would be topped off with news like this, and
suddenly the words *holiday magic* swirled through his mind.

Holiday magic?

He froze. Sara. Oh, God. Sara was waiting for him upstairs. He glanced at his watch, and his heart sank. It was
two minutes until midnight. He'd never make it in time.

But he was sure as hell going to try.

He set his champagne glass on a nearby table and hurried through the crowd, excusing himself right and left,

then brushing past a waiter with a tray of champagne glasses, nearly knocking everything to the floor. He ran into the lobby and straight for the elevator, pulling Sara's note out of his pocket as he ran.

Room 617.

He tried to stuff the note back in his pocket but missed, and it fluttered to the floor behind him. He reached the elevator, hit the button. Paced away. Paced back. Hit the button again. Waited ten seconds and stabbed it again.

He checked his watch. One minute.

Damned elevator!

Spinning around, he spotted the stairwell. He raced over to it, ripped open the door started up, taking the stairs two at a time.

Six flights. He only hoped he could make it in time.

THE MASS OF PEOPLE in Times Square undulated like a human tide, and the closer it got to midnight, the wilder the crowd became.

And the more despondent Sara became.

This had been a stupid idea. She was acting like some kind of teenage girl with a crush. Nick was here tonight on business, and she'd expected him to come up here at midnight just to give her a kiss?

She kept looking toward the door, trying to hang on to a shred of hope, all the while knowing if Nick wasn't here by now, he wasn't coming.

This had been stupid. *Stupid.* She'd spent a hundred and fifty dollars on a hotel room on the off chance that Nick could get away long enough to give her a midnight kiss? How crazy was that?

And then the ball was dropping.

Ten...nine...eight...

Suddenly Sara heard a knock. For a split second she froze with surprise, then leaped up from the bed and ran toward the door.

Seven…six…

Another flurry of knocks.

Five…four… She looked out the peephole.

Oh, God! *Nick!*

She fumbled with the chain lock.

Three…two…

She ripped open the door. He swept her into his arms and backed her against the open door.

One…

The instant a roar went up from the Times Square crowd, Nick's lips landed on hers, kissing her hard and fast, ringing in the New Year with the kind of passion Sara hadn't known existed until a week ago and now she couldn't get enough of.

As the opening notes of "Auld Lang Syne" began, his kiss became softer and sweeter, lingering as the song played, and then he eased away millimeter by millimeter until his lips just barely touched hers. He took a deep breath, closed his eyes and let out a sigh of total satisfaction.

"I can't believe you're here," he murmured.

"Didn't I tell you I wanted a midnight kiss?"

"But I never expected this."

"I thought you weren't coming."

"Things were wild down there," he said. "I couldn't get away until now."

"I know this is crazy. But I just wanted to be here. We have almost no time left, and I just wanted to—"

He covered her words with another kiss.

And that was when she heard the camera click.

19

NICK SPUN AROUND, shocked to see Raycine Clark at the edge of the elevator lobby, her photographer standing next to her. He snapped another photo. Then another.

"Raycine!" Nick shouted. "What the hell are you doing?"

Sara wrenched herself out of Nick's arms, a look of horror on her face. "Raycine? Raycine Clark?"

"That's me, sweetie," Raycine said. "And I do believe you're Sara Davenport?" She turned to Nick. "Wow. You got the syndication deal and the girl, all in the same night."

"Sara, get in the room," Nick said.

But Sara was frozen in shock, and he had to take her by the shoulders and guide her inside. Then he pulled the door closed and strode up to Raycine. As he approached, she turned to her photographer and told him to scram. The man took his camera and headed for the stairwell. Nick wanted to stop him, but what good would it do? Raycine's words were every bit as wicked as a photograph, and she'd just gotten an eyeful.

Nick stopped and glared at her. She held her ground, staring back at him with a smug expression.

"Nick, I'm so hurt. You lied to me. You told me nothing was going on between you and Sara Davenport." She sighed dramatically. "If you can't trust your friends, who can you trust?"

"Don't run that photo," Nick said sharply. "I mean it, Raycine. Don't do it."

"Now, Nick. We all have our jobs to do."

"How the hell did you know I came up here?"

"I saw you tear out of the ballroom just before midnight. Looked kinda fishy, so I thought I'd follow. And then you happened to drop this."

She held up her hand, fluttering Sara's note in her fingertips.

Nick bowed his head and spit out a curse.

"The elevator came right as you headed for the stairwell," she said with a smile, "so we got up here just in time."

"It'll ruin her career. You know that. If you have any heart at all—"

"Come on, Nick. You should know better than to appeal to an organ I don't have. But don't worry. What's bad for her is good for you. I just caught you in the act of being Nick Chandler. Those syndication people are going to know they did the right thing tonight." She gave him a little wave with her fingertips and headed for the elevator. "See you around, Nick."

He wanted to stop her. Do something—anything—to keep her from printing that story. But he knew her. He knew her tactics. And he knew there was no talking her out of it.

He ran back down the hall to the hotel room. He went inside to find Sara tossing her gown aside and yanking on a pair of jeans.

"Sara? What are you doing?"

"Getting out of here."

"No. Not yet. We have to talk about this."

"There's nothing to say. I played with fire, I got burned. It's as simple as that."

Her words were tight and clipped, almost matter-of-fact, but he heard the anger and humiliation bubbling just beneath the surface.

"I tried to talk her out of it," Nick said. "But there's no stopping her. That photo will run."

"I'm well aware of that." Sara grabbed her sweater and pulled it on, refusing to look at him.

"God, Sara. I'm so sorry—"

"Why?" she snapped. "Why are you sorry? This wasn't your fault. It was mine. I was the reckless one. I just spent a hundred and fifty dollars for a hotel room so I could have one kiss from you. How stupid was that?"

"It wasn't stupid. You just wanted to see me. And God knows I wanted to see you."

"But if being in my apartment with you was a risk, coming here was suicide. And now I'm paying the price for it." She put on her shoes, then threw her bag over her shoulder and grabbed her coat. "I have to go."

She brushed past him and headed for the door. He grabbed her and spun her back around. She jerked her arm loose. "Damn it, Nick! Will you just—" All at once her eyes filled with tears. "Will you please just leave me alone?"

"No! I don't want things to end this way!"

"They were going to end soon enough, anyway. There's no place for this to go. There never was, and we both knew it."

Nick felt a surge of desperation. He couldn't let her go. Suddenly, he couldn't fathom a life in which he'd never get to touch her again. Kiss her. Make love to her.

"No," he said. "Somehow we can fix this. There has to be a way."

"Oh, yeah? Didn't I hear Raycine say that your syndication deal is a go?"

"Yes. The guys from Mercury Media made me the offer right before midnight. That was why I couldn't come up here. There was the announcement, and all the celebrating..."

"Congratulations," she said. "You got what you wanted."

"That's not the only thing I wanted."

"Are you talking about me? You want me?"

"Yes!"

"You're in syndication now. You can't stop being that guy, and I can't be seen with that guy."

"But that guy isn't me!"

"So what are you going to do? Suddenly mind your manners? Commit to a woman forever? You do, and there goes your livelihood. Your career is built on being the bad boy, and mine is built on avoiding them. Only now I don't have a career anymore, do I?"

She tried to open the door, but he reached over her shoulder and put his hand against it. "Sara, stop! *Please!*"

She let out a breath of frustration, then slowly turned around. The most profound look of hurt and humiliation and sheer despair came over her face, and the sight of it twisted his heart.

"Sara." He inched closer, moving his hand to her shoulder, then to her cheek, and when she looked up at him, he saw the tiniest bit of indecision in her eyes. She seemed to sense the chink in her own armor, because she turned away, her jaw tight, as if she were about to cry.

"Are you telling me," he said softly, "that if I follow you home tonight and knock on your door, you won't answer it?"

She turned back, her green eyes swimming in tears. "Of course I will. I wouldn't be able to stop myself." She swallowed hard. "And that's why I'm asking you not to."

Nick couldn't believe this. It really was over.

She turned away and opened the door. Then she paused, and Nick felt a surge of hope that maybe she wasn't going to walk away after all.

"You know, it was the strangest thing," she said, a false laugh ringing through her tears. "For all my logical approach to this, for all the warnings I gave myself, for all the times I told myself this was for one week and no more…" She paused, her eyes glistening with tears. "It still didn't stop me from falling in love with you."

She left the room, the door swinging closed behind her. Nick just stood there, stunned, listening as her footsteps faded away. He put his hand against the wall, staggered by her words. Had she just said she loved him?

For a long time he just stood there, trying to comprehend it. Didn't she know how crazy that was? A woman like her falling in love with a man like him? Sara could have any man she wanted—a sharp, stable, responsible man who she could be proud to be seen with, not some radio hack who might make the big bucks but did it in all the wrong ways.

He sat down on the bed and dropped his head to his hands. He couldn't stand this. He couldn't stand the fact that her life was going to be ruined because she'd fallen in love with him.

Because he'd fallen in love with her, too.

20

Seems Boulder's number-one bad boy was even badder than usual on New Year's Eve. Nick Chandler disappeared right before midnight from a swanky New Year's Eve gala at the Brownleigh Hotel to head upstairs for a secret tryst with none other than Sara Davenport, author of the self-help book, Chasing the Bad Boy. Nick's on-air nemesis is now, apparently, his off-air playmate. Seems the guru of good girls has been chasing a bad boy of her own. Any New Year's resolutions, Sara? Maybe swearing from now on to practice what you preach?

It's a safe bet that Nick's irresistibility will thrill Mercury Media execs, who just finalized a deal with him to put his show into syndication at the beginning of next month. Rumor has it that they paid big bucks for Nick Chandler's particular brand of wit and womanizing, and after his New Year's Eve antics, it looks as if they got their money's worth.

SARA DROPPED THE newspaper to the sofa beside her, feeling so humiliated she didn't know if she'd ever be able to leave her apartment again. The story was bad enough. The photo was worse. Just knowing that right now the entire city of Boulder was looking at this made her sick to her stomach.

"I've read it three times and it doesn't get any better," she told Karen. "I haven't got a clue what to do."

"Now, don't panic. Just let me think." Karen paced across the living room, her hand to her forehead.

"Okay. We'll say that you certainly know the difference between a little New Year's Eve fun and a lifetime commitment. That you never thought of Nick as anything permanent, and that it can be empowering for a woman to have an occasional fling." She turned and paced the other direction. "And we'll say that of course it's smart to have that fling with a man who has no interest in committing for the long haul. That way, you're both on the same page and nobody gets hurt." She turned back around. "That actually sounds kind of noble, doesn't it?" .

Sara closed her eyes with a sigh, every kind of heartbreak imaginable going through her right now.

"Oh, hell, Sara, I'm thinking on my feet here. But trust me. By the time your publisher gets wind of this, I'll have something worked out."

"And what about my clients?"

"I'll put out a press release. And you can talk to them when they come in. Explain what happened."

"If they even come back in. You don't have to pretend, Karen. I know what I'm up against here."

Karen sat back down on the sofa, her brow crinkled with concern. "You know, you're kind of worrying me. Having an affair with a man like Nick Chandler? Taking a risk like that is not really like you."

"I know." Sara rubbed her temples, her head pounding.

"So why did you do it?"

Because I was dying for a man who makes me feel alive. Who is exciting and unpredictable. Who turns every molecule of his attention to me and makes me feel as if I'm the only woman on earth. Who drives me wild in ways you can't even imagine. And I wanted those things as much as I wanted my next breath.

She looked up at Karen. "I can't begin to tell you."

Karen gave her a look that said Sara was a little deluded but she loved her, anyway. "I'm sorry. I'm sorry this had to happen."

So was Sara, but not entirely for the reason Karen thought. Right now, there was something worse to Sara than losing her career, and that was losing the man she loved.

THREE HOURS LATER, Nick sat in his office at the station, staring at the newspaper, wishing he knew a way to fix this mess. He'd held on to a faint thread of hope that he'd open the newspaper today and read something else in Raycine's column, but there it was in black-and-white: a photo of him and Sara in a clinch, and a story to go with it that was filled with cheap shots. He could only imagine how Sara must feel right now.

He's started to call her about a dozen times today. But in the end, he'd decided that it was her association with him that had caused this problem. Did he want to make it an even bigger one?

His show started in forty-five minutes, and undoubtedly his listeners would be all over this. But not a thing he could say would change the fact that he and Sara had been caught together, and her reputation was going to be ruined because of it.

His was going to survive just fine.

Ted sat in front of Nick's desk, his booted foot resting on the edge of it. "You need to stop moping around, kid. There's nothing you can do about this."

"It's going to kill Sara's career."

"Yeah, she got bitten by this, but it was her choice to do what she did."

"It was our choice."

"Semantics. These things happen. People mess around who shouldn't be messing around, and they get caught. It's unfortunate that Sara's going to bear the brunt of it, but she's a big girl. You don't need to be worrying about her like this."

"I do if I'm in love with her."

For the count of five, there was dead silence in the room. Nick didn't think he'd ever seen Ted so dumbfounded.

"What did you say?"

"I said I'm in love with her."

Ted gaped at him. "You? In *love*? You gotta be kidding me."

"Do I look like I'm kidding?"

He stared at Ted, hammering home his point. Finally, Ted slumped with resignation. "Well, I'll be damned. How did that happen?"

"Hell, Ted, how am I supposed to know? It just happened. That's all. It just…" He paused, then spoke softly, "Happened."

"Never thought I'd see the day."

"Neither did I. But trust me, Ted. That day is here."

"Oh, boy." Ted gave him one of his rare sympathetic looks. "So I guess this really is a problem, huh?"

"Yeah. A big one." Nick picked up the newspaper. "Because of *this*, her career is ruined, and I'll never be able to see her again. To top it all off, I'm going to have to go on my show this afternoon and have my listeners tell me what a cool guy I am for seducing her." He slapped the newspaper back down on his desk. "God, I *hate* that."

Nick felt a shiver of dread when he thought about going through the next several years listening to that kind of crap from his listeners, and he wondered how he'd ever ended up doing that kind of show in the first place. For several months now, he'd just been going through the motions, but it wasn't until he met Sara that it had started to become clear to him what a different man he'd become.

Suddenly, he thought about being at his parents' house on Christmas day. He remembered looking at Brent and feeling a little jealous, but not because of the money his brother made. Brent had what he didn't—a normal life with a nice wife and a kid on the way. And what did Nick have? A syndication deal where he'd have a truckload of money and nobody to share it with.

He was thirty-one years old. Was he still going to be doing this when he was thirty-five? Forty? Putting off having a wife and a family because of a career he wasn't even sure he wanted anymore?

This past week had given Nick his first real glimpse of what a better future could be like. Sara was the kind of woman he never knew he wanted until now but had always needed desperately. She was smart enough to keep him thinking. Beautiful enough to keep him mesmerized. And stable enough to be there forever.

In that moment, the most profound sense of clarity came over him, beyond anything he'd ever felt in his life. And suddenly he knew what he had to do.

SARA SAT ALONE in her apartment, barely able to get up off the sofa, knowing that somehow her life had to go on but not seeing a way to make that happen. Karen had left an hour ago, still at a loss as to how to handle this situation.

They were going to get back together this evening to talk about it, but Sara couldn't imagine finding a way out.

Then her phone rang, making her already-pounding head pound even more. She ignored it until it fell silent. A minute later it rang again. Finally she rose and looked at the caller ID.

KZAP?

She hit the button to answer it. "Hello?"

"Sara. It's Nick."

Just hearing his voice again made tears spring to her eyes. "Nick? What do you want?"

"You saw the paper?"

"Of course I did. It was terrible. Everything she said—"

"Sara. Just listen to me, okay? I want you to come to the station."

"What?"

"Right now. I'm on in thirty minutes."

Sara sat up straight. "You want me there while you're doing your show?"

"Yes. I'm going to be talking about this on the air, and I want you here when it happens."

She felt a stab of apprehension. "No. No way. I can't—"

"Yes, you can. I'm going to fix this, Sara."

"No. There's no fixing this. There's no way—"

"Sara? Do you trust me? Do you know I'd never do anything to hurt you?"

Sara squeezed her eyes closed. "Yes. Of course."

"Then come to the station."

"Nick, I can't be seen—"

"Just come. I promise you this is going to be okay."

"What are you going to say?"

"I can't go into that now. Just know that by the time you leave here, this won't be a problem for you anymore."

His voice was level. Reasonable. In control. But what could he possibly have in mind? She felt as if she were jumping off a ten-story building and praying there was a net.

She put her hand to her chest, surprised that she could actually feel her heart thumping wildly.

"Yes. Okay. I'll come."

"They tell me the calls have already started, and my producer wants me to go with it at the top of the hour. I'll stall if I have to, but please try to get here before two."

"I will."

"Don't worry, Sara. I've got this all under control."

She heard a click, and he was gone.

Logically, Sara knew she should stay as far away from Nick as possible. In her heart, though, she meant what she'd said. She did trust him. She was just terribly afraid that no matter how smooth a talker he was, even he couldn't get her out of something like this.

SARA CURSED the city traffic all the way to the radio station, sure she wasn't going to make it on time, and she arrived with only minutes to spare. She walked past the receptionist and straight down the hall, and when she reached the studio, Nick turned and saw her through the glass panel of the door. Their eyes locked for a moment, before he held out his hand and flicked his fingers, telling her to come in. She entered the studio and sat down, and he handed her a set of headphones.

"Nick," she said quietly, "what are you going to do?"

He didn't say anything. He just adjusted something on the console in front of him, his face uncharacteristically solemn.

Sara glanced into the booth where his producer sat. She could tell by the look on the man's face that he was surprised to see her there, which meant Nick hadn't told him she was coming.

"Nick?"

"Shh. I'm on in a few seconds."

As soon as Sara put on the headphones, she heard the music and voice-over lead-in to his show. Nick started to speak, but instead of giving his listeners a quick agenda of today's program, he got straight to the point.

"Well, it seems you guys are a little ahead of me today, lighting up the lines before the show even started. And that's telling me that a lot of you have read Raycine Clark's column in today's paper and you want to talk about it." He paused. "So do I."

Sara tried desperately to calm herself, but she was already breathless from hurrying to get here. She slid her hands to the arms of the chair and gripped them tightly.

"First of all," Nick went on, "what Raycine wrote in her column is true. Sara Davenport and I were together at the Brownleigh Hotel on New Year's Eve. In fact, we've been together quite a bit since I first interviewed her on my show."

Just hearing him admit it out loud made a shiver of dread run down Sara's spine.

"But a little more had been going on between us than Raycine ever knew." Nick shifted a little, folding his arms on the desk in front of him. "Right now, a lot of you out there are thinking I'm some kind of hero. The bad boy who seduced the good girl and really scored. And if you look at it that way, it means that you also think Sara is a hypocrite. That she's made a career out of telling women to stay away from bad boys, and yet she succumbed to me. But here's the truth. Sara didn't succumb to me." He turned his gaze to Sara. "I'm the one who succumbed to her."

Sara swallowed hard. What was he saying?

"The only way Sara could be a hypocrite is if she was sleeping around with a man whose only goal was to get her into bed and then say goodbye. But I'm not that man. To tell you the truth, I haven't been that man for a long time now, but you just didn't know it. I don't want to interview strippers anymore. I don't want to give you rundowns of women's body parts. I don't want to drink till I drop and party till dawn and have a different woman every night. I don't want to do any of those things ever again."

Sara couldn't believe what he was saying. With every word that came out of his mouth, he was saving her career.

And destroying his.

"See, if I try to keep on being that guy I'm not, this city goes on thinking that Sara screwed up. And I'm not going to let that happen. Now, I'm no great prize. Believe me. But I can tell you right now that Sara didn't hook up with a man who intends to love her and leave her. She hooked up with a man…" Nick rubbed his hand over his mouth, then held it there a moment, his head bowed, and Sara realized he wasn't talking because he couldn't talk. And when he looked up again, his eyes were glistening. "…who intends to love her and stay with her forever."

Sara was stunned. Did he say he wanted forever?

"To put it bluntly—and God knows I'm always blunt— I can have this show, or I can have the woman sitting next to me right now. And I think I've already made it pretty clear which one I want. Now, if you'll excuse me for just a moment…"

He took hold of Sara's chair and pulled it right up next to his. He leaned in slowly, mouthed the words *I love you,* and kissed her.

And kissed her.

And *kissed* her.

Sara couldn't believe this. He'd just given up everything so she wouldn't be hurt. Given up everything so they could be together. The man she thought was nothing but a careless heartbreaker had turned out to be the kindest, most caring, most compassionate—

"Nick!" Butch said. "You got dead air!"

Finally Nick pulled away and leaned into his microphone again. "Oh, and one more thing. I have a little message for Raycine Clark. Raycine, if you're out there, I just wanted to thank you. New Year's Eve was a very memorable night for Sara and me, and because of you, we'll always have a photo to remember it by."

Nick gave Sara a smile and a wink. If she thought she was in love with him before, she was an absolute goner now.

"Okay, I'm going to take a little commercial break now, and then…well, I'm not too sure what's going to happen then. I have twin porn stars sitting in the green room right now, but I'm afraid that's exactly where they're going to stay."

Nick hit a button and pulled off his headphones.

"Nick," Sara said, "your show—"

"I don't give a damn about my show."

"But the syndication deal—"

"I don't care."

"But it's all you ever wanted."

"I told you on New Year's Eve it isn't all I ever wanted. I can imagine a life without my show. But I can't imagine a life without you. You told me you love me. Did you mean it?"

"Yes, of course I did."

He smiled. "Then I've got everything I want."

As he leaned in to kiss her again, Butch burst into the studio. "Nick? What the *hell* do you think you're doing?"

"Uh…kissing Sara?"

"The second the Mercury people get wind of this, you're history!"

"Yeah, Butch. You're probably right."

"Which means I ought to yank you out of here and boot your butt all the way down the street. And that's *exactly* what I'd do, if…"

He spit out a breath of disgust.

"If what?" Nick asked.

"If those lines weren't lighting up like a runway at Denver International. For some reason I can't fathom, you've got listeners out there eating up that sap with a spoon. They can't wait to talk to you."

Nick grinned. "Oh, yeah?"

"I know I'm probably going to regret this," Butch said through gritted teeth, "but when you come back from break, I want you to pick up those calls and go with it." He turned to Sara. "And I want you to stay put, too. You've suddenly got one hell of a fan club, and I want you to answer a few calls, too." He took a deep, cleansing breath. "Now, if you'll excuse me, I have to go tell Candi and Brandi that we won't be needing them after all."

As Butch left the studio and closed the door behind him, Sara turned to Nick with an expression of pure shock.

"Uh…what do we do now?"

Nick looked puzzled for a moment, then shrugged. "I don't know. I guess we do what Butch said. We go with it."

"What are they going to ask us?"

"I haven't got a clue."

"This is crazy."

"And you're not used to crazy by now?"

She was. For the past few weeks, Nick had taken her on a roller-coaster ride that had exhilarated her in every way there was. And suddenly she realized that she didn't want it to stop now.

She smiled. "Let's do it."

A minute later they went back on the air, and when people asked, they talked honestly about what had happened between them. Then a woman called in asking how Sara had turned Nick into a one-woman man in such a short time when she'd been dating a guy for two years who refused to commit. Sara really didn't have a good explanation for that, except to say that sometimes you can't explain it. Then Nick began to talk to the woman, and eventually she revealed she was dating a thirty-eight-year-old man who still lived with his mother, which prompted Nick to tell her point-blank that unless she was interested in being more of a mother to the guy than his mother was, it was a battle she was never going to win. Sara was a little worried about Nick's bluntness, but by the time the woman hung up, Sara realized his approach had actually made the woman see something she'd refused to face for two years.

That call spurred other people to ask questions about their relationships, some wanting to talk to Nick, others to Sara, some to both of them. By the time the show was coming to a close, Sara was enjoying herself so much that she could have kept going for the rest of the afternoon.

"Well, that's about all the time we have for today," Nick said. "Whether I'll be back tomorrow, I haven't got a clue. If so, I'll see you then. If not, thank you, Boulder. It's been one hell of a ride."

Nick signed off, and Sara turned to him with a big smile. "I can't believe it. That was actually fun." Then her smile turned a little sly. "How about you, Nick? Did you feel the rush?"

"Oh, yeah. But if you tell me it was better than sex, I'm going to have to take offense."

Suddenly the door swung open. Sara spun around to see a short, intense little woman march into the room.

"Well," the woman said, "you two have certainly managed to screw things up."

"Sara," Nick said, "this is my agent, Mitzi Grant. Or, at least, I think she's still my agent. She may be harboring a few homicidal thoughts about me right about now."

"Yes. Strangulation is a definite possibility. I just got off the phone with Rayburn. News travels fast. The syndication deal is off the table. Is that a surprise?"

"No," Nick said. "No surprise."

"Confirm for me that you've lost your mind and have no intention of looking for it anytime soon."

Nick shrugged. "I can see how you might look at it that way."

Mitzi fumed for a moment more, then took a deep, calming breath. "Okay. I guess that means I'll have to take this truckload of lemons you've dumped in my lap and make a little lemonade."

"What are you talking about?"

Just then, Butch appeared at the doorway, looking dumbfounded. "Nick, I don't know what the hell that was, but you two sure stirred something up. I haven't seen the lines light up like that since you interviewed Ms. Lesbian America."

"That's right," Mitzi said. "The listeners love it, so here's how we'll play it. New show. Nick. Sara. Relationship advice. She's the shrink with the technical knowledge, he's the color commentator. She lends the credibility, he adds the pizzazz. Strictly a call-in show, with plenty of banter between them and an occasional monologue to break things up. There'll be some crossover demographic, plus they'll appeal to a whole new set of listeners. Take what they did today, polish it up a little, and you've got a hit."

Butch just stood there, his eyes wide. "Huh?"

"Okay. I know. Big change." Mitzi grabbed him by the arm to lead him out the door. "Let's go have a drink and I'll lay it all out for you. You think Nick Chandler alone was hot? Wait until you see these two—"

"Mitzi!"

At the sound of Nick's voice, Mitzi turned back.

"What?"

"Had you thought to consult us about this?"

Mitzi gave him a look of surprise, as if the answer was, *Why in the world would I do something like that?*

"Sara might not be comfortable with this," Nick went on. "She's never done radio before. And you can't suddenly expect her to take an hour out of every day to be in the studio with me. And there would be prep time, too. It's too much to ask of her."

"No, it isn't," Sara said.

Nick turned to her with surprise. "Are you sure?"

She moved up next to him and wrapped her arms around his neck. "You just gave up far more for me than a few hours of time every week. Of course I'm sure." She leaned in and gave him a kiss.

Butch rolled his eyes. "Oh, *crap.* This is gonna be pure schmaltz."

"Don't knock it," Mitzi said. "Schmaltz sells." She turned to Nick. "I'll call you later."

After they left the studio, Nick turned to Sara. "You'll have to forgive Mitzi. She's a little manic sometimes."

"Will she actually sell them on that concept?"

"I wouldn't put anything past her."

Sara was still in shock over all of this. "You quit your show, Nick."

"Yes."

"For me."

"For us. My career doesn't mean a damned thing to me in light of that."

Slowly Sara began to understand, because she'd felt the same way herself. "When I read that column this morning, I should have been concerned about my career. But all I could think about was that I was never going to see you again."

"I wasn't going to let that happen," Nick said, "no matter what I had to do."

Sara had once thought that the time she spent with Nick was a dream no reality could match. But that wasn't true. This was real, and it was better than any dream she'd ever had. She looped her arms around his neck, thrilled to finally be touching him again.

"Now, wait a minute," she said suddenly. "We can't do a radio show together."

"Why not?"

She gave him a sly smile. "Because it means we'd have to keep up the facade of being a committed, loving couple for a very long time, and you *know* how bad I am at make-believe."

For once, Nick didn't even crack a smile. He didn't match her joke with one of his own. He simply stood there and stared at her with those gorgeous blue eyes that had captivated her from the moment she'd met him.

"You won't be pretending anything," he said softly. "And neither will I."

His solemn sincerity brought tears to Sara's eyes. The

man she thought couldn't take anything seriously was completely serious about her.

As he pulled her close and kissed her again, she thought back to how he'd shown up on her doorstep on Christmas Eve, comforting her, making her smile, and infusing her life with the kind of magic that had captured her heart. Before that night was over, he'd turned one of the worst days of her life into one of the best.

And now he'd done it again.

If you enjoyed what you just read,
then we've got an offer you can't resist!

Take 2 bestselling
love stories FREE!

Plus get a FREE surprise gift!

Silhouette™

Desire®

**A compelling new family saga begins
as scandals from the past bring turmoil to
the lives of the Ashtons of Napa Valley, in**

ENTANGLED
by Eileen Wilks

(Silhouette Desire #1627)

For Cole Ashton, his family vineyard was his first priority,
until sexy Dixie McCord walked back into his life, reminding
him of their secret affair he'd been unable to forget.
Determined to get her out of his system once and for all, Cole
planned a skillful seduction. What he didn't plan was that
he'd fall for Dixie even harder than he had the first time!

DYNASTIES : THE ASHTONS

A family built on lies…
brought together by dark, passionate secrets.

Available at your favorite retail outlet.

Silhouette Desire

Don't miss the first story in

Dixie Browning's

new miniseries

DIVAS WHO DISH

These three friends can dish it out, but can they take it?

HER PASSIONATE PLAN B

Available January 2005
(Silhouette Desire #1628)

Spunky nurse Daisy Hunter never thought she'd find the man of her dreams while on the job! But when a patient's relative, sexy Kell McGee, arrived in town, she suddenly had to make a difficult decision—stick to her old agenda for finding a man or switch to passionate Plan B!

Available at your favorite retail outlet.